ASPEN TO MANHATTAN

A Noir Affair

G Marshall Johnson

Copyright

Johnson Publishing Group, Inc.

338 S. Sharon Amity Road, Suite 240

Charlotte, N. C. 28211

www.gmarshalljohnson.com

Ordering Information:

Quantity sales. Special discounts are available on quantity purchases by corporations, associations, and others. For details, contact the publisher at the address above.

Orders by U.S. trade bookstores and wholesalers. Please contact Your Publisher/Distributor: Tel: their phone numbers or visit their website

Printed in the United States of America

Publisher's Cataloging-in-Publication data

Johnson, G Marshall

Aspen to Manhattan : A Noir Journey/ G Marshall Johnson.

p. cm.

ISBN 979-8336563344

Mystery Supernatural Travel Adventure

Table of Contents

Table of Contents

Chapter I

Rachel, my housekeeper, tried hard to be on time. She always did, but there was a little game between her and I. Rachel always showed up 15 minutes late, no matter what. I always told her to be there 15 minutes ahead of time.

Rachel had come into my life after the death of my wife, Leigh. Leigh came down with one of those diseases with no cure, and her quick passing left a void in my life. Leigh died early, but I was left with the love of my life, my daughter Elizabeth. Elizabeth, the child of my first marriage at 18, was now an adult and married, which was her life course. I was a little lonely, but it was always an adventure with Elizabeth and her husband, James. It also seemed there was a baby on the way.

"There he is," she thought.

Rachel thought her 54-year-old boss was suffering depression from the loss of a long-term mate and transitioning to his new life without his daily breakfasts with his daughter.

But Rachel wondered why Mr. Zach appeared in such a good mood lately, and then she realized something was going on as he had scheduled a trip to Denver. Why was his demeanor upbeat? She could only guess why. The pandemic raged worldwide. The nightly news was as depressing as she had ever heard it. Thirty-six-year-old Rachel was between two of her many careers. Something always went wrong for Rachel in the 8-5 jobs she held. Recently, Rachel had to move back in with her mother, and her mother constantly made her aware that Zach would be a catch for her. Rachel was not seeing or feeling it. Zach had to be in his 50s, and she still enjoyed her occasional young man.

My morning was going south fast. Rachel was late as usual, and it's her habit. I guess I could make an issue of it, but Rachel was a reliable worker, and Charlie loved her. Charlie, my golden retriever, greeted Rachel. Charlie could charm the devil- his smile and dog face reminded me how fast things can change. A few months ago, I was dogless. I can't imagine a day without his goofy smile or the energy he brings to the household. In a few short years, he would be gone. Maybe Charlie will be replaced by another homeless animal looking for love. The process repeats many times in a person's lifetime, but only once for the dog.

I waited for my driver to take me to my helipad. The AW119kx was waiting. The helicopter flight to the international airport was only 24 minutes. I live on one of the highest mountains in the Appalachian Mountain range. I use the helicopter for my East Coast travels and could only think of one thing at the moment:

I was seeing Mirabella.

I live in my family's mansion. The house was an appropriate lodge style. The views are unbelievable and within a gated community. I protected my 26-acre estate with a security group. I enjoy sunrises over the Mountain and spectacular sunsets with sunny day views of Charlotte, the South's most gracious city. Over the years, I added amenities, including a 9-hole golf course and a heated Olympic pool. The original home had been razed long ago, and the estate was not included in state or county real estate appraisals. This is another benefit of my heritage. The enhancements continued with a 345-degree view of the peaks in the Blue Ridge mountains. A two-story waterfall also graced the entrance to the home with a 3000 square foot party pavilion and guest house. I took pride in my home.

Inside my home, the woodwork is intricate with cypress paneling, poplar, and cherry that complement the intricate stone masonry. The lodge has a 25-foot-high timber-framed great room, an enhanced gourmet kitchen with custom cabinets, and a mesquite dining table. The reading room, my favorite place, resembled the Vanderbilt's library in Asheville. The mountain was a family gift, as was the surrounding territory handed down for generations.

Still, the landholdings were immense through trust and territorial agreements. The English Lord Proprietors had established ownership with the King of England, and the land grant from King Charles was massive. The Lord Proprietors were eight Englishmen to whom King Charles II granted, by the Carolina charters of 1663 and 1665, the joint ownership of a tract of land in the New World called "Carolina." George, his sixth great-grandfather, had been the only person who retained title to the land awarded, so the name and family acquired a vast tract of land in perpetuity. My family received an allodial title gifted to his family for all time. Many areas listed officially as government-owned are part of my family's landholdings. The lands stretch from the Atlantic to the Pacific.

The Carolinas, now marked North and South Carolina, have three distinct areas: "the Coastal Plain, Piedmont, and the Mountains. I had chosen the highest point in the Appalachians to view the land for my home. While remote, it had all the available amenities and served the purpose of having few visitors.

Chapter I

Today, my thoughts were only on one thing.

I was seeing Mirabella.

Chapter II

The private airport in Charlotte is adjacent to the international airport. My private car took me there in a matter of minutes.

The diaspora reeked in the airport. The staff of the private airport knows how to cater to those who want to move in luxury. I had purposely decided to fly commercial airlines. I wanted to see those things of nightly news—the nightmares of travel needed to be experienced, and I wanted to see them, feel them, and see the look on the faces of those still traveling. History needs to be witnessed.

International Airport

The International Airport was a scene of nothing. A diaspora hung in the air. There were few people and no delays or technical problems. I made my way through the travel protocols and was sad as the only other time an airport had been like this was 9/11. The day that changed America and the world forever and resulted in thousands of lives lost across the globe.

Why was I so determined to travel to Denver? The immense amount of fear in the world forced me to move. Fear never stopped me from defying the norm. Einstein said, "Nothing happens till something moves." My world had to change.

The plague and pestilence continued to devastate mankind in proportions not seen since the Spanish Flu in 1919, affecting the industrialized world. Some people thought it was created in China because of chemical and biological warfare development and that, somehow, a virus escaped. Then, people in Wuhan, China, began to get sick with unknown pneumonia, which proved massively infectious. The G20 nations, acting in unison, changed everything in everyday life. Third-world nations barely noticed at first because they don't travel to the extent of the First World, and their general health is worse, to begin with. It's hard to tell if a patient has Covid, Malaria, pneumonia, or any of a dozen other respiratory illnesses. Only the miraculously available Covid tests could tell for sure.

Schools were closed from kindergarten to university. Face-to-face meetings were allowed for only "essential personnel, "and Zoom meetings were all permitted by the mandate of state governments. Restaurants closed except for takeout. Movie Theaters were closed, and shopping malls were empty. Governments put travel, social intercourse, and life in "lockdown," possibly a warning of future restrictions. The countries of the G-20 brought air travel to a standstill due to the lack of demand and fear of catching the virus. No one wanted to be near a stranger, and the media exacerbated this fear every night.

The United States, followed by the European Union, established a welfare system of government payments. People claimed unemployment and were given additional subsidies by the Federal and State Governments. Many people earned twice as much as they did when working full-time. Many families took in thousands per week without working or a place to spend their income. What a plan! The government established a new working method as new mandates stopped everyday commerce. Except for essential personnel, all offices in the US were closed by the term "abundance of caution." Large corporations virtually shuttered their office buildings. Retail real estate prices crashed as residential prices soared.

The American economy and the industrialized world had put tens of millions out of work. Most businesses and governments mandated face coverings. People cowered in the streets in fear of their neighbors. Office buildings became vacant, and the sense of depression was heavy. It came out of nowhere. The feelings of a world gone beyond bizarre were all around.

Chapter III

Fate is an unusual lover.

Then, during the worst news and depression, I opened an email. I was surprised to receive an email from Mirabella without prior notice or expectation.

The email was from Mirabella, an intimate friend from the past. A special lady I knew in New York long ago. We had a torrid but disjointed friendship and were lovers with the passion of youth. We shared only a little serious intent. We traveled to Canada, Colorado, and New York, experiencing youthful joy when the world was more straightforward. We overcame all obstacles through our attitudes and energies.

Over the years, now over 25, she came to me from out of the electronic void. How much could I read into a hello? After a quick Google search and analysis, I found she is now an executive and a significant player in the new world of Generative AI.

Mirabella and I met at a Library convention in Chicago 27 years ago. I was a fledging sales professional in publishing. The terms of my trust required that I work independently until I reached 45. Before passing on the fortune, my family wanted to ensure my health, intelligence, and work ethic. I soon discovered Mirabella's comment about "coolie wages" was valid. Even then, she was a force to be reckoned with, and I had kept her in my mind because she possessed a passion for living that only a native New Yorker has.

The last time I saw Mirabella was at her wedding. I received an invitation, which was a surprise. Given our previous intimacy, the invitation was an odd request, yet I was on my way to my first Jewish wedding. Interestingly, at least in her home, Mirabella was from a devoted Catholic family, but she fell in love with a Jewish man. Their wedding was traditional, lavish Jewish, and Manhattan was the perfect setting.

During the social times on her wedding day, I was fortunate to speak to her for a few minutes and, more importantly, meet many of her family. Specifically, her father, who is a second-generation Italian. He seemed quite out of place in all the grandeur and was an interesting character. He carried the grace and the honor of a working man. He was a gentleman and soft-spoken. We talked, which allowed me to get to know him more deeply. More importantly, it gave me a deeper insight into Mirabella. Her family origins were from Hungry when the Italian empire controlled the region.

My former love was having the day of her life, and she still captivated me. My travel companion and I left a little early, and the next event was on an Event Boat in the East River for dinner. It might have seemed inappropriate for a man from the South to be so invasive to this scene. Mirabella looked as happy as I had ever seen. My emotions were mixed. I was pleased for the woman I had loved but saddened that her love was no longer mine. My travel companion sensed emotional roil, and she held my hand and spoke softly as we left. I was still amazed at being in Manhattan at Mirabella's wedding, but my companion soon made me forget my concerns. Time passed, and soon, it had been 25-plus years since I had been face-to-face with Mirabella. The wedding was our last encounter.

Mirabella's email came through a business forum, and I responded, which was undoubtedly an arms-length beginning. However, the email stirred all kinds of thoughts.

Her email said she had a home in Colorado and an apartment in Manhattan. She was now "working from home" and staying in place, and she was in Colorado. After a quick flurry of emails and a few brief discussions, I contrived a business trip.

My business was mostly pointless, but the opportunity to see Mirabella was too compelling to be ignored. And so, the drama began. Mirabella said she would brave the "new world" and meet me for lunch in Denver. Her comments were a bit esoteric, and we discussed old friends and catching up. I thought how amazing an electronic beam could change his world.

Mirabella

In retrospect I'm not sure why I sent the email. It's been years since last we spoke or saw each other. I've had a husband and children since then, I'm a different person than he knew then. But I guess it's like going to a high school reunion. The itch to see how others turned out is too strong to simply scratch. And there is that one thing that he has that others don't. the one thing I need now that I haven't needed before.

Meeting in Denver is not so difficult. I have the place in Aspen to retreat to if it goes badly, or even if it goes well. Meeting on neutral ground is a good idea for both of us. I may change my mind but for now I'm looking forward to seeing him again.

Chapter IV

Denver Colorado

As I arrived in Denver, all sorts of reality came to me.

The Plague was driving everyone batshit crazy. Husbands and wives had triple the time together. How many divorces will be coming in the next five years? Children and kids were at home ALL THE TIME. Masks were mandatory for everyone, everywhere. No preschool, no place to hide, just being ordered by the Governors of 50 states to stay in place and see the nightly horror show of the CDC telling us of the end of the world. The plague had hit the world. Nothing will be the same in the future.

I have tried contacting Mirabella over the years via business platforms and email. Mirabella has never responded. Once I was in the Denver airport, there were no problems and no people.

The trip into Denver was without incident, and I was grateful that when I arrived, I could find a very convenient Uber driver who quickly drove me 20 miles into Denver.

I thought: "Have I ever noticed my Uber drivers? They are all unique." This Uber driver was quite a character. I could not help but notice his earrings: I think they called it ear gauging. The car was relatively new and clean. As many of us do, I engaged the Uber driver in dialogue. He talked about moving to Denver only to have the plague cramp his business, i.e., Uber. He was married to a Hispanic lady, but he was an Italian guy from Long Island, and we discussed the cultural, social, and other differences he had found. Yes, he had arm tattoos, but none on his face. The gauging on his earlobes was much like many African Tribal ornaments. These things were the size of silver dollars, but as he explained, he was in Denver and doing his life. He mentioned he needed all the work I could give him and hoped I would continue to engage him.

 The driver was the best; he became my new chauffeur for my brief stay. Upon arrival at the Ritz and checking into the hotel, the staff seemed sad. The level of energy in the hotel was gone. Few people were moving through the lobby.

In the heart of downtown is the Ritz-Carlton, Denver. The Ritz staff was entirely professional, but the aurora of the business had changed. The desk lady helped describe what was open.

I've never seen the 16th and 17th St of Denver without life. The only people moving about today were those who lived on the street. None of the local offices were open, and to put into some mental perspective, I felt like I was in a sci-fi movie gone wrong or at least poorly written. The weather was dreary and cold, which only exacerbated the gloom.

The following day was made up of doing miscellaneous business chores. The anticipation of seeing Mirabella was all I could think of. But. as has become the custom with her, texting with Mirabella and a brief call, we settled on meeting at Latimer Square.

Rioja

The weather was raw. Cold and windy. The Ritz recommended Rioja, and my first memory is of the warmth of the brick oven. The warmth of the brick oven at Rioja, recommended by the concierge at the Ritz, was a welcome counterpoint to the raw, windy day. Mirabelle had texted that she was running late, so I ordered a red lentil soup for both the Indian flavors advertised on the menu and the warmth of the dish. It did not disappoint and stimulated taste and olfactory senses with its subtle heat, the creamy raita garnish with mint, and the explosive crunch of the base of dried, roasted, and flattened rice grains.

When Mirabella arrived, it was as if time had stopped. She was the epitome of New York chic, dressed for Denver—the style she possessed before had only increased over the years. We exchanged quick smiles and an Italian cheek kiss. Mirabelle feigned a lack of appetite and then ordered a Wagyu tri-tip and rice bowl. It was delicious as there wasn't so much as a grain of rice left at the end of the meal. I'd hate to see her when she's hungry.

We sat inside by the window. The place had only a handful of customers, and we took time and reflected on life. She told me her story of the past 25 years. She brought out the pictures from her wedding all those years ago. She was amused as she looked at the faded photos to remember me more meaningfully. It was funny when she said, "You must have been important to me back then?"

Her directness would always intrigue me.

We talked.

She and her husband Jacob had two children. Two boys. They reared their family in Switzerland and London. The children had graduated from college and were moving into career mode. One was finishing Medical School, and the other decided on a different course as an officer in the military.

Mirabella had worked for an international bank and found numerous opportunities that came her way. Jacob worked as a financier for a private trust. His clients were both in the US and Europe.

In her manner of storytelling, it seemed she had repeated this tale many times, and she shared the "fight" she and Jacob had made to save his life. He had a disease that was not curable. For six years, they fought the good fight. They made trips around the world to make every effort to cure him. The trips to the US and European clinics were exhausting, leading to her eventual acceptance and pain. And yet, she did not seem to be emotional anymore. After Jacob, Mirabella had to get on with life. Family and Career now dominated her life.

"My boys had grown older, with similar career paths. My daughter married and sat firmly on the "Mommy" track, "said Zach.. The conversation stayed in a very "old friendship" way. Friends catching up during a "crisis" in the world. For me, it was an unforgettable day.

I found out her mother was still living in New York. Who knew? Mirabella had two overly complex sisters whom I met at her wedding. She had a love-hate closeness sister thing going on.

Jacobs's illness was not a point I wanted to dwell on. Mirabella seemed to have compartmentalized her thoughts and the story. It was better to leave it. Mirabella had preternaturally beautiful eyes. The intensity and the humor she projects in her eyes are persuasive. Her eyes have a hypnotic spell. When she focused her gaze on a person in her sphere, her subject felt as though they were the only person in the room, the only person Mirabella had ever met and the last person she would ever need to meet. Twenty-five years, and the eyes still captivated me.

We picked up as if no time had passed. Mirabella recently moved to her new home in Colorado, and now, with homes in New York, London, and Colorado, she had concerns about selling a home in upstate New York. I assured her that remote, well-maintained homes were now commanding a premium. The world outside our restaurant had gone wild, and we did not run out of conversation for almost two hours. The more we talked, the closer we became.

For a minute, I remembered Mirabella's claim that she'd never been to Aspen before. With a nearby house, I wondered about her claim. I was just about to ask when I had a memory that burst out of me, and without thinking, I asked.

"I remember your hands. May I see them?" Mirabella held them out.

One morning in Annapolis after a weekend together, twenty-some years before, I remembered her in the early morning. At first light, her hands were draped across my shoulders. The hands were those of a goddess. Long and lean and without imperfection. This memory of Mirabella's hands has never left me.

Quizzically, she smiled as she placed her hands in mine. Being the quintessential New Yorker, her nails were perfect, and her hands rolled back time. It appeared the nails were manicured in a unique shape that was intriguing. I laughed to myself as she sat beside me in the restaurant. The restaurant may have four other patrons, but we had the place to ourselves at this window seat. The gray day outside conspired to keep a soft light on us. It was as if the old friends we once were had last seen each other only a few weeks before. Strange and highly caring, Mirabella had the unique ability to blend time. She showed that everything started to come together, from being an Italian mother to a close friend. As time began to extend, we both knew it was time to leave. We both seemed to know there would be more on leaving the restaurant.

Mirabella

I was lost in thought. I had a grand luncheon in the middle of the Pandemic. Leaving the restaurant, I thought about how it could be after 25 years that we were so comfortable with each other.

What brought us together now?

These were circular questions and a quandary. I would think more about it, but I had to return to the new house and my army of handymen.

It would be interesting to see if I could regain control of him as I once had.

I need to keep secrets for my own reasons. I believe Zach has forgotten much of our time together.

Zach was of this world, and my world was "different."

It may be interesting to "play" with him for a bit in a good way.

Zach did not remember things on many levels. It was a sharing we had done long before, and he may not have realized it had occurred. I thought of the others who have come into "my world," Fortunately, because of my learned actions with people of this time, I knew, as did "Dorian Grey," they would all change. This time, this place and Zach seemed suitable for... I suddenly realized he was about to ask an inconvenient question. I had him change the subject.

Eventually, our lunch ended, and we air-kissed goodbye with the assurance that we would "do this again soon." Mirabella's Uber arrived, and I watched her leave my life again—this time, who knew how long the gap would be. Denver in late October is cold. The wind blows, and it seems even more chilling without people. With the evening open from any social obligation and Denver closed. I decided to stay in. I had dinner at Elway's in the hotel lobby.

Steak.

Chicken.

Salmon.

I chose steak. A great Cabernet from Napa was suitable for the wine.

Chapter V

Back to Denver International

My Uber driver became my valet during this trip. No one was using Uber very much, and he was kind enough to offer assistance on several occasions; most importantly, we scheduled a pickup for him to take me back to Denver International. Upon entering Denver International, the response to the plague was the real story.

The airport was a ghost town.

No People

The TSA checkpoint had more employees than passengers, and if you know Denver, they have a TSA set-up that looks like two football fields in length. Seeing that one of the world's biggest cities and economies had no traffic was terrific and intimidating. There is a certain peace and anonymity in being part of a crowd. With so few people in the terminal, I stood out in uncomfortable and disturbing ways. As nearly the only person in sight, TSA stared at me hard and long.

The flight back to Charlotte was uneventful and getting back into the shuttle to the private airport felt safe in this world that had seemingly turned upside down. Rachel was calling from home and was concerned about when I would arrive. She had a different agenda than Charlie and me.

"Rachel, I will be there in 45 minutes."

I could tell from the change in her voice she'd found an event for the evening and was self-satisfied with her plans. Although she didn't say so, I figured she had a date for the evening. I hoped she had a good time.

Summer

The months passed, and Mirabella and I texted, talked, and caught up on our lives. The backdrop of the end of the world nightly news was daunting; the plague had seen a continuation of the apocalypse promised by the CDC. The Pandemic was frenzied. The nations of the G20 seem to be determined to close off the world of commerce. The American economy was continually brainwashed with nightly news, which would only remind those old enough to remember the body count daily in the Vietnam War. The third-world nations began complaining that needed drugs and supplies were only going to the rich nations. The rich nations acknowledged the issue, but nothing changed in the third world.

Tens of millions of Americans were out of work. Public Schools and Universities closed. As the Work-from-home trend continued, critical and essential personnel were only allowed into offices. As the Pandemic raged, at least on the TV screen, it was simply a touch of a science fiction movie gone wrong. Nothing opened up as the months went on. Doctors' offices introduced telemedicine. Conglomerate Health Care will always find a way. All the national media emphasized was how COVID numbers were nothing in comparison to the Spanish Flu but:

Travel stopped. Trains and Cruise ships halted. Amazon became wealthier. The Port of Los Angeles locked down shipping, leaving dozens of container ships waiting at anchor offshore. Worldwide supply chain issues grew astronomically. Surprisingly, there was no food scarcity or fuel scarcity; prices soared, and the sleeping public began to awaken.

Russia declared war on Ukraine for the second time in ten years. In response, America left hundreds of thousands of weapons in Afghanistan as they claimed victory and pulled out. In Syria, the civil war continued, awaiting the upcoming Israel/Hamas war, which was in its planning phases.

Masks were mandated for use in public. Everyone had to wear masks everywhere. Everyone except the elite who were "exempted" for various reasons. New medications first went to the wealthiest communities and then trickled down to the masses. The first vaccine was supplanted by a second, with a third promised. Meanwhile, promising medications not on the government dole were refused and denied.

Fear was rampant- older people were considered high-risk, and hospitalizations skyrocketed. Essential health equipment grew scarce; protective gear became the standard by which value was now judged. Sanitary supplies sold like crazy. Some entrepreneurs decided to charge scalper prices for basic needs. The best of mankind reared its ugly head as the daily count of infections was skyrocketing. However, deaths were minimal compared to other pandemics, but the news made the end of times appear near. News outlets were making money in amounts unseen since 9-11. The head of the CDC was a nightly fixture on the news as he tried to convince people that the government knew what was best.

With all things dark, Mirabella and I became advocates for each other. Our Mental health was challenged by nearly everything, but we discussed and planned our next adventure.

27

I impetuously suggested that we could meet in New York immediately. At worst, I could drive to the city from Charlotte avoiding all of the Pandemic protocols. I wouldn't have to deal with Masks and or distance regulations. But, it would take a day's driving and all that entails. Mirabella is worth it though. There would be far more to do in New York than in Charlotte, although I would love to have her come and visit. But she seemed reticent to renew the relationship, whatever that now was. I pressed gently but met resistance each time. My frustration grew with time.

Chapter VI

For several months, Mirabella and I continued our conversations by text as she preferred. We discussed potentially getting together again and visiting. We were two friends talking long distance. After a while, conversation slowed, and nothing substantive occurred for several months. Our conversation went back and forth during the holidays- Happy New Year, and everyone was ready for the resumption of a "normal" world. People hoped the pandemic fears would ease, and this would be the year things became more routine, and everyone was just generally hopeful. It was merely an illusion of hope. The terrible reality of things continued.

Mirabella had frequently traveled between Colorado and Manhattan to manage her affairs in New York. The lack of airline passengers did not concern her. "I value the time alone without outside interruption," she said. She educated me on the new, experimental Retina Scans in airports and how the bacteria level on the scanners far exceeded that of any other airport surface.

Will we dance?

In every long-distance friendship, things either advance or end. Summer was coming, and we chatted about Colorado and my preference for Durango and the four corners.

" Mirabella, have you ever been to Aspen"?

Mirabella said, "I have a home near there."

"Have you ever been on a balloon flight?"

I was trying to find an enticement. Surprisingly, she had never been on a morning balloon flight, so I mentioned the Hotel Jerome. She'd heard of it. We went a bit sideways on this one. In the past, authors and people of note were regulars at the Bar in the hotel. The tradition continued to the present. Mirabella was not as intrigued as I was. I kept looking for things that would make her at least interested in coming. Then, after issuing a challenge to her, things changed. She was not one to avoid anything. It was as if time was becoming necessary to her, and our time together had created some urgency.

We were meeting in Aspen!

Mirabella

I haven't been to my Aspen home in over a year so Denver is a good place to meet. The stunning natural beauty will be a nice change from Manhattan's grey and stodgy buildings. Things are going slowly in New York, mostly do to the Pandemic protocols. Broadway is shut down, everyone is wearing a mask or staying home. The life and vitality of the town has been sucked out. This is what I imagine Soviet era cities were like. Who would have ever thought that a bank would be happy to see masked customers enter their premises? Yet it happens hundreds of times a day as people try to continue their normal lives in abnormal situations.

I've seen it before, but this time it comes with the added burden of tyrannical government intrusion. Demands to get unproven shots, distance yourself from friends and loved ones, and restrictions on travel and companionship have reached a level I've never seen before and hope to never see again.

Aspen will be a nice break, if only for a weekend. And, if I play my cards right, I can get what I need from Zach.

Chapter VII

Trip to Aspen

The Flight from Hell

Rachel surprised me by arriving early. She had started expressing undue interest in my comings and goings. Rachel was curious.

"There is a bit of a question in my mind," she pointed out. "I've noticed you are traveling a bit more now. Want to tell me what's going on."

"Just new business opportunities. Now is the time to get busy."

Rachel knew me well. In her mind, she shouted, "I knew it! There is a woman involved."

The copter ride to the international airport was uneventful. My pilot, Charles, was used to quick trips at a moment's notice. I was grateful his family lived on the mountain, and he knew most of my quirks. There was a little difficulty in transit at the beginning of the journey. Because of the news, I wanted to see what the world looked like now compared to my earlier trip to Denver.

The flight plan was for American Airlines to travel from the Charlotte International Airport to Phoenix, then a short flight to Aspen. It appeared there was enough time for plenty of delays. However, the International Airport was a little bit busier in August.

To the airport, I went. The plane for Phoenix was delayed, so I missed the flight from Phoenix to Aspen. I had that moment of anguish that everyone has. You are busting your ass, running to the gate, and that fatal moment of realization that the plane is pulling away from the entrance. I cursed about "my absolute frustration with the Airline Gods."

The kind people of American Airlines then advised me that they have only one flight per day to Aspen, which will be tomorrow afternoon. The leap of faith required to trust the airline was not that strong. I felt my best impression would be made by being patient.

As a sign of the times, the restaurants in Phoenix airport were closed. No, not one, all; they closed at 3 p.m. The airport felt sad, as if you wanted to eat after 3 pm; you were SOL. I thought, "Who knew they only have one flight to Aspen daily from Phoenix in the summer? Who trusts airlines these days? Only those with unlimited time to spare." It was a harbinger of the future.

I decided, "Well, that wouldn't work because of the timeline." Mirabella was on for the weekend, and nothing was going to interfere.

I resorted to begging the people at American Airlines. I booked a flight to Denver on United Airlines. On paper, it could work. Then, the weather gods started playing their games.

Circling Denver, the arrival of my United flight was delayed because there was a hailstorm directly over the airport, which delayed flights for two hours. Waiting for a two-hour flight meant the connection time for the Aspen flight via United was minimal. I was a road warrior in my previous life. Time to use those skills.

I decided, "Well, that wouldn't work because of the timeline." Mirabella was on for the weekend, and nothing was going to interfere.

I resorted to begging the people at American. I booked a flight to Denver on United. On paper, it could work. Then, the weather gods started playing their games.

Circling Denver, the arrival of my United flight was delayed because there was a hailstorm directly over the airport, which delayed flights for two hours. Waiting for a two-hour flight meant the connection time for the Aspen flight via United was minimal. I was a road warrior in my previous lifetime to use the skills.

I gathered my thoughts, and immediately upon getting off the plane from Phoenix to Denver. My first stop was to the gate agent.

"What gate is the Aspen flight?"

"I'm sorry. Sir, but that flight has already departed."

"I thought there was a hailstorm over the airport. How could they take off?

"I'm sorry, sir, I just came on duty; I don't know what happened."

"Ok, what time is the next flight?"

She studied her screen. "We don't have anything until noon tomorrow. But Frontier has a flight leaving in about ten minutes at gate 55."

I shouted "Thanks" over my shoulder as I headed towards the aisle, where I spotted the only person who could help. Mr. Leroy was the first person I could find with wheels. He has a great smile, and his red jacket fits the bill for a reckless ride to gate 55. I commandeered the golf cart.

"Mr. Leroy, do you want to make $100.00 in ten minutes?"

Mr. Leroy responded, "Get in."

The excitement was palpable as we rode in and out of groups of people at the gates. People can move fast when they fear a moving object in a building. It seems Frontier has something like 99 gates, so when we got to the flight to Aspen for the second time on the same day. I screamed in my mind, "Deja fucking vu," as I saw the flight pull away from the gate to Aspen.

Well, now I am stranded at Denver International Airport. Mr. Leroy was still waiting for me. Our conversation was quick. Is there a hotel attached to the Airport?

"Yes," he replied, and I hopped in to ride to the Westin.

Thank God for the Westin at Denver International.

The sci-fi experience jumped back into my face. Zombie Land was in front of me. People were lying on the floor, and the number of delayed people was beyond calculation. Descriptors are inadequate to describe the older people, young people, and kids on every bench and sleeping in every position possible. I was surprised to see so many people, given that the airport had been so empty. They must have all decided to go to the Westin. It made sense as it was the best and only hotel at the airport. Mr. Leroy pocketed his hundred and headed back into the bowels of the terminal.

People were lying all over the place; they missed their flights and would need to spend the night there. It was fast approaching midnight, and it all became surreal. Nothing ever works well in an emergency world.

"Who are these people, and why are they in my world tonight?"

Into the Westin. I continued the midnight quest for a room. I queried the desk clerk, and she smiled. It was apparent that all rooms were sold out and had a waiting list. The lady smiled a becoming smile, and being very professional, she offered a little hope. She suggested I may want to take a cab down to 10 Mile Rd; when I get down there, there are 10 or 12 hotels, and I may find something there. Thank the heavens for Uber in Denver. I found an Uber professional willing to help me find a place to sleep after midnight. Uber and I took off for 10 Mile Rd. Unlike an average Uber transaction, the driver and I agreed on an open-ended drive.

From the airport, upon arrival at 10 Mile Road, another eerie scene came from hotel to hotel.

There are ten or so hotels, and I devised a routine that, thankfully, the Uber guy was up to the challenge. Walking into the hotel and giving them a thumbs up became routine, and they would reply with a thumbs down. There were no vacancies anywhere. Now 2:00 AM. The Uber driver was very patient. We went down to another exit close to the airport, which was another five to seven miles away.

Again, there were no hotel rooms, but Providence intervened.

I walked into the Aloft, and the lady at the front desk announced.

"Well, you're in luck, and I said, " Why," and she replied, " Well, it seems a group could not get here tonight." The flight was delayed, and they called and freed up 20 rooms. "I've got one for you if you want it."

With the frustration of the day and the adrenaline still pumping, I had to rage at the world. Have you ever had the feeling of being so wired that you could not sleep? Frontier had given me a telephone number to call that would help me on the remainder of the trip. Frustration and anger about the situation did not help. Given a particular number to call by a Frontier professional, I behaved poorly and started calling Frontier Airlines and American.

The airlines were of absolutely no help. It was a low point, and somehow, it was eerily appropriate. Then I thought about how I would get to Aspen. There's only one way, and it was not an egregious trip from Denver to Aspen. The drive is about four hours. Three and a half if I push it. I decided that I would drive to Aspen. I was too wired to sleep anyway. I called Avis and called down to the front desk,

I walked into the Aloft, and the lady at the front desk announced.

"Well, you're in luck, and I said, " Why," and she replied, " Well, it seems a group could not get here tonight." The flight was delayed, and they called and freed up 20 rooms. "I've got one for you if you want it."

With the frustration of the day and the adrenaline still pumping, I had to rage at the world. Have you ever had the feeling of being so wired that you could not sleep? Frontier had given me a telephone number to call that would help me on the remainder of the trip. Frustration and anger about the situation did not help. Given a particular number to call by a Frontier professional, I behaved poorly and started calling Frontier Airlines and American.

The airlines were of absolutely no help. It was a low point, and somehow, it was eerily appropriate. Then I thought about how I would get to Aspen. There's only one way, and it was not an egregious trip from Denver to Aspen. The drive is about four hours. Three and a half if I push it.

Contrary to the problems at the airport, the rental car company "Avis" was on point. They provided excellent service; it took 10 minutes to check in and get on the road. Avis won the award for getting me out of Denver. I was not looking forward to a drive through the mountains at night after a stressful flying day. But Mirabella had called, and I could not refuse.

The drive during the summer is exhilarating. One gets to go through Vail, Colorado, and the Vail pass. The Vail pass is more than 10,000 feet. If you have skied in Vail, you know the pass is a place that can be closed due to weather. Snow during the late evening is something to experience.

The Ute Indians first inhabited the Gore Creek Valley long before settlers moved west. The valley offered a summer home for the Utes, who spent winters in the more arid lands of Western Colorado. The Utes called the majestic peaks of the Gore Range that overlook the valley "The Shining Mountains." Settlers moved west into the Gore Creek Valley in the mid-1800s, turning the area into ranching and grazing land. During World War II, the United States Army created a training center south of the valley called Camp Hale, where the 10th Mountain Division trained for alpine combat. Made up of excellent skiers and mountaineers, the 10th fought in mountainous Northern Italy. Upon return, they became major players in the quickly growing ski industry, founding or working at over 50 resorts in the U.S. One veteran of the 10th Mountain Division, Pete Seibert, returned to

Colorado skiing after the war to join the Aspen Ski Patrol and Aspen Ski School and eventually became the Loveland Basin Ski Area manager. While at Loveland, Seibert and Earl Eaton began looking to develop another ski area in the Rocky Mountain region.

The Vail village has a special aura, which only became an idea in the 1960s. With help from Denver investors, construction began in the spring of 1962. The town of Vail was founded with the resort and officially incorporated in 1966. As the resort grew, the town shared its good fortune: from a handful of condos and ski runs, restaurants, a medical clinic, and more would appear. Capitalism is a beautiful thing.

Seeing the growth of one of the world's largest ski resorts was unbelievable.

Glenwood Springs is the next exit after Vail before you turn on Colorado 82 to Aspen. I thought about my past trips to Glenwood: A more beautiful valley could not be carved into the Rockies. It sits atop the Continental Divide and splits Colorado's eastern and western parts. Glenwood Canyon has a long history with the Ute Indian tribe and was a spiritual center for the tribe. The Canyon is ruggedly scenic. It has walls that extend to a great height and is, like many images, a place that needs to be experienced. It is awe-inspiring. The Canyon runs beside a river and is worth the effort, a visual that stayed with me. I was sad that I would miss the display at this hour of the morning.

The Transcontinental railway makes an overwhelming statement to the time in the US development while overriding the indigenous Ute tribe. All I could think about was the magic of driving through such beauty at night to see Mirabella.

Indian natives of the Ute tribe were the forefather neighbors, feeling overwhelmed by the country's beauty and disgusted by the will of General Sherman and Lincoln to take land from the Indians.

However, nothing interfered with my need to see Mirabella in another hour later today.

Chapter VIII

Glenwood Springs

I had a history in Glenwood Springs-

Once, on a ski trip, I asked a beautiful girl to marry me there. Who knew if I would have ever returned to the Springs to marry her? She told me, "No," and we parted ways.

You take a turn in Glenwood Springs on Colorado 82. Then on to Aspen, and suddenly, the action began. Mirabella was texting me as I neared the town. The phone was ringing, and texting at a high level began. Great things were coming about. Mirabella was calling to confirm what we were doing and offered a solution to help me. And there was a peace about it.

Mirabella said, "Why don't I go ahead of you? I will make sure everything is ready when you get there."

It's an omen for great things to come.

Mirabella

The trip to see Zach in Aspen has been a concept and nothing more. As I prepared for my trip, it came to me, "What am I doing?" I looked at his picture in the background of my photos in the wedding album from 25 years ago. He had aged well when I met him in Denver—going to see him brought on all sorts of thoughts, chief amongst them, "Why am I doing this?"

"I have a quasi-man friend in Connecticut; while highly informal, it was there. James is a singer/songwriter who is trying to make it big. We've

been seeing each other for two years since I first heard him sing in a café in Boston. Casual yet familiar."

Connecticut does not challenge me, but it is convenient when I need an escort. "This man from 25 years ago shows up in Denver, and now I will see him for a weekend. What an interesting hold he has on me?"

I was reluctant to share with my sons as that would be a definite no-go from their perspective. How could this be happening? I knew. Turning "50" and working with a cadre of 25-year-olds somehow made her maudlin. Never one to back down from a challenge, it almost seemed as if Zach had laid down a gauntlet.

Aspen- a balloon flight- dinner, and a change of pace did not sound all that bad. I also knew myself. My sons were my life, and my career was fully operational. The plague had closed most of the world, but Colorado had a different perspective.

Manhattan is my home, and one more person seems excessive, yet I was traveling to meet someone from my past. Yes, here I am, driving down Colorado Highway 82. With plenty of space, people seemed more relaxed and lived quite differently from Manhattan. Aspen was only 45 minutes from my Colorado home, and I thought if this became a problem, I would pack my bags and go. Zach and I were not that close at this moment. I could quickly "bail" if this went south.

"Here we go," I said to myself, returning my attention to Zack. We discussed the context of our time in New York, but all I remembered was that he had crystal blue eyes, was at least 6 feet tall, and was not altogether unattractive. I hoped seeing him would trigger further

memories of long ago in him. The memories were explicit, I knew, and he had never known.

I had difficulties with my life then, and the term "hot mess" could have been applied. I chose to forget.

Zach saw me as something other than the secret I kept. Sometimes, I was very complicated and could be a selfish woman—shapeshifting from one personality to another. I sometimes imagined people's stories, making things enjoyable on the drive to Aspen. I used my hands-free controls to keep a constant stream of texts with Zach.

The texting on the drive to Aspen increased. Zach was about 2 hours behind me, and I wanted to check where we would stay.

The apartment in Aspen was in Snowmass Village. It was a two-bedroom with a cozy living area. Better yet, it was only 200 yards from the slopes. If things turned south, this would give a perfect segue to change the narrative. Sick children and everyday items came to mind.

I expect to see an exhausted man. The travel difficulties were almost overwhelming. I thought he would call the whole thing off. This adventure had little to do with Zach. It was about my need to connect and see what I would be like with a former lover.

I had forgotten the tenacity of this man.

Chapter IX

Arrival in Snowmass

After my four-hour drive, I was visually stunned.

Mirabella had expressed great concern about my trip and how I must be exhausted. Nothing could have prepared me for Mirabella. She and I were on the phone when I pulled into the parking lot.

To say I was stunned would be an understatement. Mirabella glided towards me as if lifted by the mountain air. I was nearly speechless. Hell, she flowed as if on air. Her look of care and concern was beyond my experience.

There are moments when you are taken aback. She dressed as if the designers had created a visual just for her. She flowed down the steps. Her outfit was a designer's creation. Prada, Vivendi, I had no clue.

Nothing could have been more surprising. It was as if we had never been apart; Mirabella exuded supernatural caring and familiarity that started when we met for lunch in Denver. I had no expectations. I was concerned that this adventure could go south. My expectations for the trip were nonexistent, not knowing how the next few days would go.

I am still amazed at her courage. She was away for a holiday with a man she had not seen in 25 years. As we last met, she cast what seemed to be a spell over me with her eyes and smile. The energy and clarity of her thought seemed beyond most conversations. The term sanguinaria came to mind from out of nowhere.

After settling in at Snowmass, we started our experience.

Early Dinner at Hotel Jerome.

The drive was all of 10 minutes. Parking was plentiful. The town was laid back and felt great after a long day—an oasis in the middle of the Rocky Mountains. The hotel is a square building built in 1889 that has survived the silver crash, the Depression, two world wars, and Hunter Thompson.

We ate in the dining room, which was very formal at this time and not in keeping with our vibe. Delicate wine glasses made the room perfect for this meeting. Breakfast at Prospect in the Hotel Jerome sets the tone for our day. Eschewing the $10 bowl of dry cereal, we opt for protein in Eggs Rancheros and Eggs Benedict, which should last until cocktail hour.

She was the epitome of New York chic, dressed for Colorado—the style she possessed before had only increased over the years. We exchanged quick smiles and an Italian cheek kiss. A wedding was to happen later in the day. The wedding party took over the dining room, leaving just two tables unencumbered by revelers. The couple's joy and their army of friends made for a significant change of pace from the usual dining room experience. It saved the day.

The wedding people were having a great time, and we ended up talking and meeting several people who were beginning a journey that Mirabella and I had just finished separately. Mirabella was a natural at meeting and relating to others. I, on the other hand, am always cautious. She seemed to have two personalities: "the engaging extrovert yet had a more temperate and prudent side. I spoke at length with the groom and his father. They were from a small town in Wyoming and came to Aspen for the event. We talked about cattle, grazing rights, and oil.

Mirabella decided on the fish for dinner: Colorado Rainbow Trout and Agnolotti. Later, she educated me about agnolotti. Agnolotti is a type of stuffed pasta typical of the Piedmont region of Italy, made with small pieces of flattened dough folded over a filling of roasted meat or vegetables. Everything about the lady was Italian, and she reveled in her element.

Being more plebian, I chose a dish more aligned with my heritage: Montrose beef short ribs, Colorado pinto beans, juniper red wine, celery root, carrot, brussels sprouts, beets, and chanterelles.

The taste of the beef short ribs was almost a phantasmagorical experience. It was as if the food were not of this planet. The essential taste was of a delicious light fish, and it was a consistency that complimented the dish's other elements. The beets and chanterelles made this dish an experience. The chanterelles tasted beyond a mushroom, making the dish exciting, clean, and pure.

Then we had to go into the J Bar. It was mandatory for me. Old memories flooded back as my youth crowded my present. The bar is heavy, dark wood. - It gives the impression of a powerful sense of place, resembling a western mining town. The bar stools are of the same dark wood, accented with red leather. Sitting at the bar is like riding the world's most comfortable saddle. The J-Bar is infamous in the history of Aspen. The Rolling Stone writer Hunter Thompson once ran for Sheriff in Aspen. He turned the J Bar into his functioning office. The bar has an ambiance of the old West, and the 19th-century bar remains part of the social fabric of Aspen. During my past times in Aspen, the J-Bar brought many new characters into my life. Aspen has this fantastic ability to make skiers and socialites mingle effortlessly. Legend has it that Thornton Wilder, the author, learned how to get around the ban on alcohol during prohibition. He would order a milkshake spiked with bourbon. I'd guess he was not referring to Aspen as "Our Town."

There is a place in the bar where every bartender has signed one of the walls while they worked there: an exciting tradition and a link to the past. We both opted for a bowl of soup and the Ceasar salad, saving our calorie allowance for the Apple Strudel and the Bananas Foster Parfait.

We walked down to the base of Aspen Mountain and enjoyed meeting a few people doing valet parking. They said it was not going well during the Pandemic. They were more optimistic about the coming winter season. Hope springs eternal in the heart of an entrepreneur.

Chapter X

While the J Bar exuded an old-timey, Western ambiance, the Silver City was as bright and shiny as Aspen's newest bar should be. From the galvanized, corrugated trim on the actual bar to the numerous televisions hanging on the walls, the Silver City was as different from the J-Bar as possible.

The Silver City is in the BPOE Building. The building is named for a fraternal organization (The Benevolent and Protective Order of Elk). The informality of the place is excellent—a bar area and then, to the right, a line of tables for dinner. The staff seemed glad to see us. We went into the bar and stayed.

Mirabella has a unique way of engaging the people we meet. She sits next to or in front of them, reaches out a hand to make a physical connection, and then looks deeply into their eyes. She talks softly and slowly at first, then accelerates the discussion to a normal pace, all while holding the person's gaze with her eyes. I've seen her do it numerous times, and it never fails to mesmerize her subject, much like a serpent and its prey, only with benevolence.

Her ability to make each person feel special was classic. All the people we met seemed to be induced into some trance state. Hypnosis comes to mind, but it was an easy thing for her. I am not sure she was aware of her "uncanny" ability.

The day was waning, and we had to prepare for our 5 a.m. balloon ride. Regretfully, we said goodbye to our new friends and ignored their cries of "just one more!" My sleep deprivation was showing, and I found myself losing track of conversations. It was time for bed.

But first, we needed provisions.

Clark's Market

We hadn't made any preparations for even minimal provisions. I suggested we go to Clark's Market. A short walk away from the Silver City. The walk would do us both good after hours of sitting and drinking. The cool air hit my face and snapped me into wakefulness. Mirabella slipped her arm into mine, and we started down the street.

I felt as if I was with someone I had known forever. Her arm was warm against mine, even through our clothing. We strolled along, window shopping and people-watching as if we had been together for the 25 years since we met. Maybe it was the fullness of my heart-warming our contact point.

We went to the market to get provisions. Clark's Market is like Disneyland for foodies. Artistically arranged displays of fruits, vegetables, and seafood compete with similar displays of every food category and seasoning you can imagine. We could have easily spent days at Clark's, but time restrictions and sleep deprivation hurried our selection process. Although we could have gotten breakfast at the balloon company, I wanted to take advantage of every minute with Mirabella. Fruit, coffee, and bagels for the morning seemed to be a perfect light breakfast. Whatever needs heating we can warm in the microwave in my room. Everything else could be eaten as desired on the trip or throughout the day. Clark's seemed to have everything we needed for a weekend away.

Mirabella and I were on the same page. Whether or not the familiarity was feigned, I did not care. She picked out items, and I added them. It was as if we had been to a small market when we were back in New York City light years ago. Either she had the most insightful intuition or a clairvoyant effect going on.

Because of the long travel, we'd decided on an early evening; we were probably back at our bungalow around eleven o'clock. I got my second wind on the walk from Clark's, and we stayed up until 1:00 or 1:30 in the morning, talking, laughing, and drinking wine. Things were absurdly familiar to both of us, and we talked till late evening and early morning about family and our life apart for 25 years. The wine made for an increasingly easy conversation as the evening hours progressed. The conversation became much more personal, and a sharing of tender emotions came up.

Mirabella: "Did you know I have been on my own since I was 17?"

""Really?" I replied.

"I moved out to escape my mother and lived in the basement of a neighbor's home for two years until I could get to Manhattan and school."

"WTF?"

"The man I married saved my life. When we first met and became involved, I was into the party scene in New York. Jacob is the reason for my success and for overcoming myself. It changed my life when he died, and I am not sure anything will ever come close to what we had. You probably need to know these are not facts I can see as ever-changing. "

She mentioned a scholarship in his name, but I only heard her talk about the Korner Store & Deli somewhere in New England.

"I think I've said enough for today," she concluded.

"Let's call it an evening; 5:00 a.m. will come soon enough."

5 am

We sleepily made our way into the kitchen. Coffee, some orange juice, and a bagel made it work. I made a cup of Lemon water. Mirabella said, "I did that for years. I should start again." I cut a lemon into halves and went about squeezing. Mirabella taught me a technique of how to get more from a squeeze of lemon by microwaving the fruit for a few seconds before cutting.

She stopped me and said, 'This is better." She then took a fork and inserted it into the meat of the lemon. It worked much better. The feeling of closeness and of knowing each other was almost eerie. Everything was easy.

Mirabella said, "Sorry about last night. I think I nicked you on the neck."

I had no memory of it, looked into the mirror, and said I didn't see anything. She smiled.

The 1.2-mile trip to our launch pad was easy and exhilarating, and we found ourselves at what appeared to be a park. It is cold at 5:30 a.m. in Snowmass in July. The sun is not up, and the first light begins. We dressed in layers to make it work, and with the event's excitement, it was a great moment. The adventure brought a sense of calmness as well as excitement.

The crew for our adventure was busy laying out the balloon on the ground. Two crew members held open the mouth of the balloon. The next step was to inflate the balloon. The gas-powered burners are enormous and roar like a jet aircraft when they ignite. The majestic beauty of hot air rising to fill out the balloon amazes me. Inflating the balloon took about 35 minutes; you get in the basket like life.

Mirabella was amazed at the size of the balloon. She watched the balloon inflate to over 100 feet, which made for great conversation with our newly assembled group. The conversation was difficult over the burner noise, but Mirabella entranced the group as usual.

Two crew members held open the mouth of the balloon, and it started to rise majestically. Captain Don was in his last season as a pilot.

"Is this balloon safe?" Mirabella asked.

"Most of the time," I said.

"How long will the ride last?" Mirabella asked. "How far do we travel?" she asked.

"Just to the other side of the Airport, not far, not long," I replied.

Getting into the basket is not what you think. We put one foot on the basket ledge, and like riding a horse, we swung our legs over the edge, and then, awkwardly, we were off into the morning sky. As we ascended, we could see the unbelievable beauty of the mountains around us, and the views were stunning as the sun rose. Slowly, we lifted off from the earth. We could see unbelievable beauty in the mountains, and the views were amazing as the sun rose. The flight carried us over the Aspen airport, where we got to see planes land beneath us. Captain Don enjoyed his job, and he pointed out interesting sights and told stories about the area.

Since balloons fly by the wind, they only change directions by going higher or lower to get different wind drafts. The flight carried us over and past Aspen airport. We saw planes land beneath us. Captain Don described the aircraft, speculated on their destinations, and held our attention for the entire trip.

After 90 minutes, the balloon made its landing. Today, we were fortunate to have a longer ride because of the winds and our course, as most routine balloon flights last about an hour.

We embraced the ride; the entire experience as we knew it would pass quickly. Mirabella noticed that four of the ten people were from Russia.

In the way that she bantered with them, she almost seemed to know them. The Russians were driving those huge black SUVs, of course. The ladies were young. She thought:

"The men are more mature, thinking their 40s."

They talked about Aspen Mountain, which dominates the town. The discussion of the property seemed very Aspen as all the homes appeared to cost millions, and who knew, maybe these guys were oligarchs of some type. Mirabella did notice that some discussion of Switzerland came into play. As Mirabella lived there for ten years, she was intimately familiar with the social and political realities. Mirabella, by her proclivity and work, was an investigator. It seemed improbable to her that the Russians and I knew each other. The probabilities of a meeting at dawn were, at best, minimal.

What better way to have no one listen to the conversation than in Mid-Air? "Was Zach transacting some kind of business with these guys?"

Her mind was racing, but fate and Occam's razor theory were probably the answer. "Russians in Aspen, well, who knew?" She dismissed the thought. Aspen seemed the place for eccentrics and has been eclectic since before the days of Hunter Thompson. Creating new resorts was a topic everyone had on their mind. Mirabella was a good sport about this adventure. She smiled, and I believed that was not normal for her.

The process of landing involves a chase vehicle that follows the balloon. As the balloon descends, it is almost impossible to pinpoint the landing. Landings are always exciting because you bounce along the earth in a basket. You are holding on for dear life, yet you are also sad that you're ending your flight. Did you know there is no landing spot for a Hot Air Balloon?

It then dawned on Mirabella that she may not land back at the park. Fortunately, we had a "chase car" following, and when they saw we were landing, the crew circled, and the chase car crew was on the ground to help us land. We landed with a couple of bounces, and the chase vehicle crew grabbed our ropes and pulled us to earth.

The next step after "departure" from the basket is excellent. Champagne is served. A light fare is provided, and the conversation is active. Toast, toast, and more toasts are made for the safety of the trip and a few Irish homologies. The first toast, by Captain Don:

"May you be in heaven half an hour before the Devil knows you're dead."

"Vashe zdorov'ye"

"Cheers!"

The Balloon company provided transportation back to the park via their chase van.

The "Russians" had the black SUV pick them up.

Even after our breakfast and the light repast from the balloon company, Mirabella and I were famished. There is a wonderful restaurant in Snowmass Village. It's part of a general store, or it seems that way. I think the name of the place was the Daly Diner. We'd walked over from our bungalow, and it may have been a 5-minute walk, but it was interesting to see all that was happening in the small town. Excellent outdoor seating: we sat in a beautiful setting at 11:30 in the morning with mountains in the background in very low-key traffic. We sat outside, and while they had certain dishes, I remember The Spicy Bloody Marcus, with a garden full of garnishes to the usual Bloody Mary suits Mirabelle's adventurous palate. I stick with the Classic Mimosa.

Since the plague arrived, everything has changed, and the lively town of Aspen has been trying to survive. I believe only one other couple was there for breakfast, and we had the attention of a great waitress. She gave us the scoop on the entertainment on the mountain and in Aspen. The pickings were slim.

After all of our non-stop action, we crashed. Mirabella hit the sofa and did not move for 3 hours. I made it to the bed, and with a cacophony of man sounds, I slept like a log.

Mirabella and I were engaging in a flow. Sleep during the day and stay up till the wee hours. She came alive in the evening. Her energy became more assertive, and it was a. reminder of Manhattan.

We slept.

We stirred in the late afternoon. The World Plague made everyone aware of the work-from-home option. Strategically, we became office mates. Mirabella took the table in our dining room and created her own office. I took the other end, and here we were, connected to the world by Zoom. Our business continued as it would have if we were in NYC or Charlotte.

With children and family in New York, there were the inevitable phone calls. I could overhear Mirabella on a few occasions. Her mother called, her kids called, and even her sisters. Probably making sure I was not a psycho.

Her mom called. "Hi, honey," Rose said. We have been trying to reach you all day, and you have not **answered**".

Mirabella

"I'm in Aspen with a friend," "I didn't have cell service until just now."

"Well its not like you to just disappear like this. We were getting worried."

Nothing to worry about. I'm meeting an old friend from New York for the weekend. We went hot air ballooning and have been eating our way through town."

Well don't do too much, you're not as young as you used to be."

"And I'm younger than I'll ever be again. Don't worry, this is America. Everything risk free and safe as houses. Everything is taken care of."

"I don't know," said her mother, "who is this man?"

Like I said, a friend from another life in New York."

Aspen

The evening was leisurely. The bartenders at the Sky Bar were waiting for us. There is a sense of friendliness among a particular group of bartenders and guests. We drank smoked Old Fashions as a perfect kick-off to our evening.

Mirabella asked the waiter, "How did you choose Aspen to live in?

The answers from three different servers seemed self-apparent. We ski, we have work, and this is paradise.

"Tell me more about the feel of Aspen now versus when you arrived," asked Mirabella.

The server's story was short but explained it all.

"My story started 20 years ago, living in the back of a 1998 Chevy pickup at the Highlands parking lot." Like many others, our server said he arrived with nothing except pocket change and an old pair of skis. "I soon made many friends, and they helped me find work, and it worked. I survived and thrived."

"Somehow, the magic gave me a wonderful wife and family, wonderful friends, a dream job that allowed me to compete on the world stage in my chosen profession, and a modest, comfortable lifestyle.

Mirabella replied, "Wow, you must work for the Chamber of Commerce."

After a few cocktails, we were off to Mezzaluna.

Mezzaluna Aspen opened in 1987 and is a locally owned and operated restaurant. They serve lunch, après ski, and dinner daily in a bright modern dining room, where Italian art decorates the walls.

Our table at Mezzaluna was inside. The atmosphere had an open-air feel as if outside. We chose to dine inside due to the cold exacerbated by our fatigue. The waiter was professional and knowledgeable about their wine offerings. Mirabella and I decided on a great red wine from Tuscany. As always, Mirabella and I defaulted to Italian dining when she desired.

63

Mezzaluna had been around for a while, and the service was impeccable. Even during the pandemic, the waiter was amazingly professional, and you felt like you were in an NYC restaurant.

The restaurant, we were told, is locally owned. The thing Mirabella did enjoy was the Italian art that lined the walls. I ordered an old favorite, Osso Buco, and Mirabelle got the day's special, lasagna. The lasagna noodles are freshly made and delicate, with just enough substance to support the bechamel and Bolognese layers of the dish. I'm hoping she can't eat it all. My pork was tender and delicious, and the braising liquid perfectly paired with the creamy polenta. The service was warm and friendly. Our conversation turned from convivial to a severe tone.

"Mirabella, may I ask you a question?" I asked. "Do you know who I am?"

Mirabella shook her head, "No

"I could tell," I said.

"I had a period of my life that was dark. We discussed this in Denver. I was involved with drugs, and that was when we knew each other; the best I could remember," said Mirabella.

"Wow, you are spending time with someone from an old wedding photograph,"

"That would be true," Mirabella agreed.

"Well, I hope you have been pleasantly surprised," I said, trying to feel her thoughts on the weekend.

" Beyond any expectations," she said, reaching for my hand.

Mirabella was a great conversationalist, but I knew she would be an excellent person to have discussions with. Her business savvy made for interesting conversations. She mentioned during dinner that we both have times when tough negotiations are part of our world.

"Isn't everyone's," I responded,

We discussed different ways to approach tough negotiations, and then, from nowhere, she asked, "Are you familiar with the work of Schopenhauer?"

I was stunned and then realized she was either querying me on philosophy or had a more direct point.

She said, "There is a book I think you will like. It is about 45 pages long and is called The *Art of Controversy*. Written in the 1700s, it points out three ways to argue."

Schopenhauer

She then proceeded to discuss the three ways. Our discussion was a fantastic articulation of the current political situation, which resulted in a riot in the US capital. Who knew? Two hundred years before, the dynamic of dialogue was the same.

Mirabella said, " Let's get out of here, and we can talk back in Snowmass."

Mirabella began by talking about her unique ability not to remember past events but to have particular memories of the recent past. She discussed it as an ability she possessed. The power was unusual in that she described it as trance-like. She could, at times, seem to take control of people. She seemed to know their thoughts and desires, even memories on occasion.

In her meetings worldwide, she discussed the collective unconscious - the collective conscious. The part of the mind that may create archetypes and primordial images. Not consciously but innately in humans around the world.

When Mirabella spoke, her eyes became even more captivating. She seemed to take over both our presences. I thought she must have been trained in hypnosis and even been an expert in induction techniques. As we talked, I felt she could read part of my mind. Mirabella could somehow control the human mind, thoughts, and memories. It was almost as if she could hypnotize at will.

We had a past, and it seemed she had a convenient memory of our time together, and I had a sense of something not quite right. It was as if I wanted to follow her without her talking.

Our day was energizing. It was approaching 11 p.m. when we set off to Snowmass. Our quickly formed custom included the opening of a great red table wine. The conversation was relaxed.

"Our time is passing too fast," Mirabella said.

"What shall we do about that?" I asked.

"Would you think me forward if I asked you a question?" Mirabella began.

"Not at all."

"I don't get many days like we are having. Family, work, and the world seem to have gone into hiding in Aspen."

"Why do you think we are here?"

"Aspen is as good a place to escape the world. Let's stay through the week."

Confused as only a complete surprise like this could bring. "Why?" I asked myself. My mind raced. Without any reservation, the only answer was:

"Yes"

The following day, we started more deliberately. It only takes a few minutes to figure out everything going on in Aspen. We became regulars at the Snowmass Village breakfast deli. Breakfast began at about 11:30 am. By noon, we had read the local paper, perused the local websites, and plotted our day.

The days passed with a tremendous unexplained speed. Sleep during the day and stay up till the wee hours. There seemed to be a flow that Mirabella and I were getting accustomed to. She became alive with the evening. Her energy became more potent, and it was a reminder of Manhattan.

Mirabella

Zach's face lit up like a Christmas tree when I suggested we stay the week. It's clear that I am having the desired effect on him. Maybe tonight I will get what I need.

Chapter XI

Day trips

Mirabella was again dressed in a unique vision of a high fashion model on the cover of an REI catalog or the magazine "Outdoor." Her fashion sense seemed to be in every element of her look while maintaining an eminently practical approach to exercise. The colors and her style set her apart from everyone we met along the way. She was simply a knockout. The nuance of all her styles took me away.

Crater Lake

We hiked. The destination was Crater Lake, which is a few miles from Aspen. Crater Lake was at an altitude of about 6,400 feet and was reached by a downhill hiking trail about two miles from Maroon Lake; Mirabella noticed we were in the White River Forest.

The most revealing point for me was the stamina that Mirabella had. Since I live in the mountains of North Carolina, I'm somewhat used to hiking at elevation. Mirabella matched me stride for stride.

She said, "I walk everywhere in Manhattan."

The elevation of Aspen is around 8,000 or more feet, and we both became a bit winded during the hike. The beauty of a mountain lake in the Rockies cannot be described. This lake has unique characteristics as it changes in size with various seasons. We saw waterfalls and noticed even a few leaves changing. The water has a tremendous blue-green vision. The sky is clear. It is not East Coast clear, but Colorado clear. The lack of pollution is beyond description unless you are a regular in western Canada.

As for me, a mysterious countenance was all over my mind. It seemed that Mirabella and I were back in our late 20s. Mirabella possessed great strength and stamina; for some uncanny reason, normal fatigue was gone, so it seemed for both of us.

I also noticed that Mirabella had the body of a much younger woman. Her face resembled someone in her 50s, but it seemed either fate or nature had been very kind.

I asked myself, "What is it that I don't know? Was it too early to ask?" Something in our relationship nagged at me. Mirabella was the same person physically that I remembered from all those years ago. Something about her demeanor was different. She was older, of course, but also there was an aura about her that I didn't remember. Something was different but I couldn't place it.

"I would like to go to the Aspen Art Museum," Mirabella said.

"Sure. Did I mention you have a penchant for visiting museums everywhere you go?" I replied.

"I certainly do. I have memberships at many Manhattan museums. The Metropolitan, MoMA, and the Guggenheim are a few of them," said Mirabella.

"Tell me why you find this such a curiosity," I said.

"In Europe, you are surrounded by history, and I have become a devotee of seeing all the best things that have been around since we started," said Mirabella. "There is a familiarity about these places that has attracted me forever. Seeing all that has been since recorded history began is fascinating, and I knew you would be interested."

"Why?" I asked.

"In our telephone conversations, your knowledge of the US and its history and philosophy let me know what you appreciate. I also remembered our time together years ago. Finally, I think you would do almost anything I ask."

"You know me too well. Let's get something to eat." We both laughed and headed for the Diner.

After our traditional late breakfast, we went to the Aspen Art Museum. Outside of the museum is a fantastic view. It incorporates a Western but contemporary feel.

An exhibit and auction were the features of the week. "Art Crush 2023" featured more than 40 artists and an array of visuals. Art seems to define the summer in Aspen. Artists were the focus of our brief time in the museum. It seemed like a summer gala, a phantasmagorial experience of Painting, Sculpture, and Photography. OK, we spent nearly three hours in the museum. We left tired but mentally refreshed. The museum had a small restaurant and ways to imbibe.

Mirabella had mentioned her son might be thinking of a destination wedding, and we found out from the locals there was a place in Aspen well known for these events. The time continued to rush, and we went to the Little Nell on one excursion.

Her son had recently finished medical school and found a lady. Mirabella and her son realized that the lady (Katy) and her family shared the same strong work ethic they held. Mirabella said she liked Katy as she was driven to develop her advertising firm. The two families seemed to merge effortlessly, and Mirabella now had the daughter she never had before. I could see the pride and love in her eyes when speaking about them.

Mirabella was also "tireless," I could only see a rosy future for this young man in the middle of such amazing feminine energy. The couple had known each other for a year or more, and the timing seemed right. Katy was also ready to begin her next life stage; children were essential to her.

At 8,000 feet above sea level, the view at Little Nell is a beautiful setting for such an event. It would be a perfect destination wedding.

On a later side trip, I interrupted our plans. I told Mirabella I once met the singer John Denver in Aspen when he took his kids to a movie in the 90s. They have a new memorial dedicated to John. Stones by the river with parts of his songs etched into them. It seemed very appropriate and was touching. Yes, Aspen is small enough to accommodate such things.

The memorial in Aspen is near Theatre Aspen's summer shows. It is a wonderful place, and they also have the lyrics of many of his songs etched into river boulders. The song "Rocky Mountain High" had to be inspired here. While my cosmopolitan lady from Manhattan may not have been overly enthusiastic about the subject matter, she tolerated my whims for a few minutes.

Mirabella

The idea to spend more time together surprised me as much as it surprised Zach. I could have ruined everything before it even began, but we spent our time hiking, walking, visiting museums and eating our way across the mountains. WE exhausted ourselves every day and enjoyed our evenings together.

Chapter XII

"Belly-Up" Aspen

The musical groups performing at the Art Crush were numerous and diverse. I knew some but did not know others, like Deadmau5, Pat Green, and The Maggie Valley group. We felt it interesting given the diverse music scene of the town.

Mirabella thought about how many things we could do in a few days. Every afternoon, they had local live entertainment. The same crowd showed up, and as the waitress invited us to the breakfast restaurant, it became "friendly" to our routine.

In Snowmass Village, a small bar was still open. It had a name from the New York scene light years ago. "The Limelight." It seems improbable, but two Aspen/Snowmass area hotels have similar names. The closest Limelight was in Snowmass village, and they were the only place to have live music. The other Limelight had not opened yet. A boutique hotel was coming next year.

They featured local talent as the state of the world demanded. This summer season with live music was still an anomaly because of the pandemic protocols. The Lounge had folk and jazz groups playing. The crowd was small, but we danced for the first time on our trip. The locals were into this, and we did not restrain ourselves.

Mirabella was surprised at the quality of our 5 p.m. watering hole. The Limelight captured her imagination, and we returned multiple times. The stage is small, and the atmosphere is more comfortable. Everyone was over 45, and all that implies. Short, tall, thin, and otherwise, but the conversations' conviviality made the atmosphere work. The people made the place.

Mirabella and I walked everywhere. She is from Manhattan and did not even think about distance when walking. When I met her light years before, she explained that New Yorkers walk to keep themselves fit. New York has two types of blocks. Long and short. The blocks on avenues are about 8 to a mile, and the others are much shorter, about 10 to a mile.

The village of Aspen is only 30 by 30 blocks. It allows for a pedestrian street mall, which is easy to navigate, and there seem to be only a few town street names that make it easy. There is Hymen Ave or Restaurant Row and then Main Street, which leads to the base of Aspen Mountain. While it may take a few minutes to get used to the directions of things, it is certainly not a very large town, and from one end to the other, the drive may take 15 minutes at most. Walking can take as long or as short as you want.

What is impressive is that Aspen has Transit Authority buses running from Snowmass Village to everywhere in town and the surrounding hotels and condominiums. It was the dead of summer, and the buses were running like it was the winter snow season. The whole effect was of a peaceful respite in a world outside that seemed so confused. This place has a soul that makes things seem so solid.

We continued to tour Aspen. Music is a driving force in Aspen, and Jazz is part of the Aspen experience. We heard music from several venues. It seemed music was playing all over the downtown area of Aspen. The park at the center of town seemed to breathe life.

The servers told Mirabella and me that Sheryl Crow, Stevie Nicks, and Eric Church would come to town in the next few weeks. Who knew that this place was so alive with these talented artists appearing?

Our time seemed to be running out fast, and we had to decide what to do next to augment our impromptu adventure. Mirabella wanted to know everything about Aspen. We took a guided tour of a neighborhood to view the architecture. We reveled in our role as tourists. Aspen has a West End neighborhood that runs along the Roaring River, and our guided tour gave history and detail to the town's architecture and development.

Tourist mania continued with us. We took gondola rides up Aspen Mountain. The Gondola ride is a fantastic way to end a day. The views are without comparison. The nights were a bit of a haze. I could have been under the Mirabella spell or seemed like a dreamlike haze. I continued to feel strange in the mornings and had a tough time remembering the night after we returned to our room. It didn't matter; these things happen as we age, right?

In personal moments, I was mesmerized by Mirabella's scent. It was as if all things of nature came with her. At first, I thought it was simply perfume, but it was more visceral. Her scent made the trance-like state increasingly pronounced. The smell and taste of her was mesmerizing.

As time passed, her taste and touch would bring about an excitement I had not known in years. My mind seemed sharper, my muscles seemed stronger, and my libido shot through the roof. Overall, Mirabella was a connection that seemed so familiar and comfortable that time blended into a transcendent closeness. How could we be so close and not have been together for all these years? The following weekend was upon us, and we did a good thing on our last day.

Mirabella

Our time passed too quickly. It had been decades since I behaved without regard to the clock. We became entwined without effort. I may have made some concessions, but why not?

He is a good travel companion. I did find his conservative, almost libertarian views a bit much, but he seemed to have transcended the need for argument with me.

Zach seemed to be connected to the country and the land in a traditional, old-country manner. The land was something to be held and cherished, not to be exploited like a ripe fig. His reverence for the history and substance of the land showed through his personality and presence. Maybe it was due to his family history as guardians of their granted landholdings. Perhaps it was a result of years of living in a rural area. He was refreshing from my usual companions.

It seemed he was part of the historical past, especially the geography, wherever we went.

I thought of the dangerous game I was playing. His invitation to my wedding was purposeful, and I cannot even confront that issue within myself. When we reconnected on the Internet, I nearly moved on without action. I think that now, I'm glad I reached out to him.

The remembrance in my mind is clear. His time of existence is so limited. Some things are beyond the understanding of "mortals." Some things are best left alone, she thought. I learned this concept early by being different.

It seemed our trip was ending too quickly. Mirabella was the consummate take-charge lady and told me to get my butt to the airport without long goodbyes. I was disappointed that we would be separating and going on our individual ways, who knew for how long this time. The uncertainty of it all weighed on me through our goodbyes. I tried to put on a brave face and hugged Mirabella farewell.

Then, as if an afterthought, Mirabella asked:

" What do you think about Manhattan for the fall? It is only weeks away if you are up for it."

I thought this was much more than I had hoped for.

"What dates are you thinking?" I asked.

"Broadway is opening up, and we should be the first to see a show." She said.

"Let's see what shows are open," I said, smiling to myself.

Aspen Airport-

The Aspen airport is about a mile from Snowmass. The rental car return was more accessible than any place on earth. We chose the valet option and turned the car over to a young lady who whisked it away as we entered the terminal. The airport has an air of efficiency; however, the seating is Airport 101. The airport has five gates with only two commuter flights during summer. We only saw one small group leave.

Interestingly, two gates seem to be for private planes. These are jets, and one of the parties boarding was from Los Angeles. At least the apparent giveaway was the cliched ladies and their dresses. If they were not texting, they were chatting. The men had had enough of their female partners and drifted to one end of the airport while the ladies were all over the place. The "eye candy" from LA was not a bad way to end the Aspen week. But I didn't seem able to concentrate on anyone but Mirabella.

All good.

Mirabella.

Zack was enthralled with Aspen. He called it a "found Oasis." It was, to my taste, way too WASP-ish. Zach was with his people, it appeared. Being of Italian-Hungarian descent and having been schooled in diverse environments, I was a bit taken aback at the feel of this place. It was almost too perfect. The people all looked great, and there was a feeling that everyone was wealthy. Manhattan was my home. The city had everything anyone could need and was available at a moment's notice. Nothing was inaccessible from Uber to Taxis and private cars if you could afford it.

I had two mindsets. One was the girl who went to school and knew the city well. The other was the woman I had become. Outwardly sophisticated, world traveler, and now this? What was this madness I was entering? The truth may come to us, but what could it hurt for a few weekends? I had secrets that transcended the modern world. I must make sure that this would fit. If not, I must tamp down this burgeoning romance and return to my normality.

Manhattan would be easy for me. I suggested Zack get a hotel with a conference room as he wanted to work while in the city. It would be acceptable to keep him away from my home, especially if he had any clients or old friends coming by. Zack understands my world without being conscious of his knowledge, but he only knows a part. I invited him to the wedding for a reason, and he may never know why. Zach would have no reason or way to understand.

Chapter XIII

MANHATTAN

Autumn in Manhattan

The First Weekend

The summer passed quickly for me. Mirabella and I emailed and talked often building a reservoir of commonality that was missing in our first go-around. I learned so many things about her life in the past 25 years. How she met and married her husband, the lives of her children, her business life bloomed over the years and made he a wealthy woman. I learned of her current friend in Connecticut and her family's lives and achievements.

I shared with Mirabella the same events and milestones. I'm sure my information was boring to Mirabella given her glamorous existence in New York. I looked forward to our time in New York with growing anticipation. Finally, it was time.

The weeks of autumn in New York are magic. Our proposed week in Manhattan was five weeks in the future. Mirabella and I continued with effortless elegance in our long-distance relationship.

Being apart from Mirabella was difficult. I found myself to be not as sharp mentally. My muscles ached, and my joints protested at the slightest provocation. Rachel had become flirty, but it affected me not at all. When I compared myself to my Aspen self, the difference was stark.

My trip involved flying into Westchester and taking 40 minutes to ride into Manhattan. I had not told Mirabella of my travel arrangements as they involved items of which she may disapprove. I took my private jet (a rental, actually) into Westchester, and the implied snobbery of the overuse of resources was not on her present agenda. The experience of flying into NYC and not being involved with LaGuardia seems the only terrific way to go.

My hotel was the Downtown Marriott. Not the fanciest, but centrally located and stocked with multiple conference rooms I could use for the business I needed to conduct. Mirabella and I would meet up in the lobby at noon. This gave me plenty of time to check in and get ready.

The world continued in chaos. The trip to Manhattan was seamless enough. The picture that everyone has masks on was a visual distortion that cannot be understated. The government mandate still existed, and the airport and security were all hampered by masks. NYC created an app for your COVID card and entry to public places. Face covering had been historically done only by thieves, and maybe the thievery was being conducted on a larger scale under the color of authority. Still, there was no way to stop the train from leaving the station now.

Checkpoints:

The government called it the COVID-19 Vaccination Record Card. I got mine when I received my first vaccine injection. As boosters were given, the card was updated as needed. The card is made of simple cardboard and signed in ink. It was dated and stamped.

In Manhattan, you could buy a covid card anywhere on the street. People who need to interact with the public need a COVID card. If you did not believe the CDC's pronouncements of vaccine efficacy, you needed to get one somewhere else. There is a thriving business in fake COVID cards ranging from about 50 dollars on up. Where else could this happen? Capitalism strikes again. It did happen, and if you wanted to travel, you had to have the "credentials."

Mask mandates were in all public places. It is eerie to feel so isolated in Manhattan. The economic effects of the continued restrictions have been impossible to ignore. Lockdowns are leaving workers out of their jobs. People were buying fewer items. Taxi and Uber drivers noticed that there was no traffic. Business "work from home" became an area of contention as many of the New York firms said:

"If you want New York pay, you must come to work."

The pharmaceutical industry was promoting and testing various methods, but getting used to the utter arbitrariness of the pandemic is impossible.

Mirabella came up the escalator like a roman candle. He vibrant outfit caught the eye of men and women alike as she strode across the room. I enjoyed the sight for a minute before I stood and waved. She made a bee line to me.

"There you are!" she said.

"And there you are" I replied.

We hugged and air kissed. We were in public after all. We took a few minutes to catch up on my travel and her trip to the Marriott.

Mirabella invited me to her apartment. "I want to show it to you." She lived in the Sutton Place part of town. Her building was built in the

1800's. It was in a cul-de-sac, and the street ended and overlooked the East River. It may also be the only place in the US still with pay phones. The doorman at the Apartment was a classic vintage style. He was older, somewhat stooped, and gnarled. He eyed me up and down before his eyes gave way to a mysterious look. He called Mirabella and went with me to her apartment door by way of an elevator from the early 1900s. When he pulled the metal grating across and engaged the lift, it seemed he was doing so for a lifetime of work.

Protective of Mirabella, maybe? Protective of the building, for sure. It seemed the doorman had many roles, but I felt he was more of an overseer, controller, and observer and had seen most things that would ever come through the door and how to deal with them.

I looked into Mirabella's eyes with great anticipation since it had been weeks since our summer trip, and you never knew what would happen in a few weeks.

Mirabella

My thoughts ran on a random pattern. I was not excited but anticipated the next few hours. Aspen was one thing. This weekend was another. Zack would be in my home. The place where I shared my business and life with family and friends. Which was Zach to be? Or would this be a fateful end to a bad idea? It was a leap for me and, in many ways, much more intimate than Aspen.

I am confident of my ability to control Zack. There was an Outlier here, and I am still fearful of it. If things go too far, the spells could be reversed. I would be the one being controlled, and that could never happen. The secrets are much too large. There would be a disaster of proportions not seen since the European events in her family.

Mirabella's apartment

The building seemed ancient. The view was outstanding: The East River and the ever-present Pepsi-Cola sign. The interior design of her apartment was Cosmopolitan Chic. The space was well done and compact—white leather sofa with color explosion above in a framed print. The coffee table and art were well placed, with an ottoman under the window. The rug was a tree design, maybe with red accent colors circular or just plant leaves exploding with a dash of color. A picture of Mirabella's sons was appropriately placed, and the artwork was surprising.

Interestingly, she had African Art objects. She seemed to have artifacts from Benin City (Nigeria). The art has been sold and displayed in the world's top museums for decades. I asked about one, and she said, "A Bena Lulua figurine." I had no clue.

As we discussed her career, I found her current business discussions were a passion. Mirabella was the ultimate AI professional. Her knowledge of databases, search engines, and startup companies was encyclopedic. I got a college education in Artificial Intelligence sitting on the white sofa.

The kitchen was well-appointed and had the unique items of Manhattan. The stove and the other appliances were ultra-small, giving the illusion of space. The kitchen must have been upgraded as it had hardwood floors, chrome chairs with leather seating, and all the white and chrome appliances. A splash of vividly colored marionettes accented the walls.

The living room still had a unique part of Manhattan. There was a window unit air conditioner. It had been years since I had seen one. The apartment had vividly white walls spoiled only by the color of the rug and the look of a high-end hotel. The white leather sofa and the essential big-screen TV were pulled together by the carpet that brought gray and red with muted circles and an off-white base color in a designer fashion. I, as always, looked for the water closet. Surprise. I have not seen anything so startling white in years. It almost made "operating room" standards.

Mirabella's bed was queen-sized, which may have been her preference when alone. The room changed its visuals as the pictures on the wall above her bed were all Charcoal drawings instead of all the colors in the other rooms, and I wondered why the change.

It was terrific that we picked up where we left off so effortlessly. I felt at home with Mirabella. I noticed her fingernails first; they were dark maroons. The shape of her fingernails had been altered slightly, and they looked a bit more pointed. I was now in Mirabella's inner sanctum, although it appeared somewhat corporate.

I felt like I was in the quintessential New Yorker single female apartment. Everything seemed completely normal. Why was I uneasy?

Chapter XIV

We fell into the comfortable pattern we'd developed in Aspen. Our days were spent walking the streets of New York inhaling the sights, sound and smells of the city. We enjoyed sights big and small from the Intrepid Museum to a small park where children ran screeching at each other. We laughed hard and often. We spent walks strolling in silence just watching the human carnival parade around us.

La Villetta

The food of the various cultures made the world seem like our hometown. We decided to go for an early dinner at La Villetta.

This neighborhood restaurant made for the start of a great weekend. The staff seemed to know many of their patrons and were on a first-name basis with Mirabella. The interior of the restaurant was a classic Italian restaurant. White tile floors, wooden tables, and chairs with a white tablecloth covering. Photos hung on nearly every square inch of wall space. Actors and politicians from an earlier age stared out at the living as if judging their level of enjoyment. We decided on two antipasti plates instead of a main course and ordered the frito misto and the mussels in white wine. The mussels, squid, and shrimp on the frito misto platter are just enough protein, and Mirabella has the mushrooms and zucchini on the frito misto platter to herself.

We chose a great seat on the outdoor patio to enjoy the fall atmosphere. The service was impeccable and friendly and had the professionalism of an authentic dining experience.

I wondered if the world would ever return to typical from the Covid epidemic. Having dinner in New York was always an immense pleasure, but it had been inconveniently altered during the pandemic. Fear is a mind-killer. News reports began to come from people worldwide being driven into their apartments, and moving to our Western states was terrific.

Broadway

Opening Night

The first weekend.

We made our plans to go to Broadway. Broadway had been closed for a year. Dark, as the New York Times would say. The excitement was palpable. With no Broadway for a year and COVID card requirements, it took a lot of fortitude to brave a theater crowd. We were going to see:

Chicago

Ambassador Theater

219 West 49th Street New York, NY 10019

Mirabella commented on a couple seated in front of us. They had decided to dress formally for this initial Broadway opening. This couple wore more formal clothes. Dressing for Broadway was a distant memory, and in front of us was another young couple. The lady wore a beautiful cocktail dress, and the gentleman wore a tuxedo. As they tried to take a selfie, I intervened and asked if I could take a photo of them. They were ecstatic. She was beautiful, and he was handsome, just like the 1950s had made the look famous. But in front of Mirabella and me, he was a living example of New York Broadway style.

Chicago had been running for a zillion years, but it was still Broadway. The story brings together a chorus girl who kills her lover to advance her career. A shyster lawyer from the Chicago heyday of gangsters turns the Chorus Girl into a celebrity. The lawyer had never lost a case involving a female defendant, but his fees were very high. The lawyer demands payment in advance or exchange of money from promotions and rights to the case. The lawyer defends two clients and wins both cases.

The dancing, the music, and the power of a live performance can make you understand why this show has made it for 25 years. You can feel Bob Fosse all through this production, as it is a musical with great laughter and cynicism. In the theater, the world was still mask oriented. But that night, it opened a world of beauty.

My masked Mirabella, with her scarlet red jacket, looked beyond compare.

230 Fifth Rooftop Bar

After the show, we wandered over to the 230 Fifth Rooftop Bar. The view from this location is stunning. The Empire State Building lit like an Art Deco Christmas tree in one direction. To the left is the New York Times building, and to the right is the New York Life building. Sprinkled in between are constructions of greater and lesser import and impact. The overall view is one of transcendent Capitalism and boundless optimism.

Manhattan's sight and feel on a fall night are seductive—the view of the bridge and Brooklyn from the other side's viewpoint over the East River is astounding. As we entered, the nightlife was fully engaged. The ladies of Manhattan have no peers regarding style and attitude. The big drawback to the crowd this evening was the presence of masks hiding half of everyone's face.

Admittedly, in our 50s, we may have been a bit out of place by the numbers, but I remembered why Manhattan has always been the first choice for fashion, desire, and romance. Mirabella held her own with the ladies of Manhattan. I was also taken aback when she seemed to control the waitpersons—instead of waiting, she commanded a presence that dictated the staff to favor her. I had noticed this behavior in Aspen. She had some hypnotic control she could use. We chose our seats outside to enjoy our evening.

The walk home

As the long day neared its end, we made the short trip to Mirabella's home. The gate's guardian, the ever-present doorman, awaited our arrival. While walking back to her apartment, the world seemed to slow down. Our evening ended late, and again, a strange energy took over. Physical and Mental energy became alive as the evening grew longer.

Mirabella had a unique technique of using her nails on my back late at night. It was almost as if she had a unique expression of arousal. It had happened before, but the intensity was changing. She never mentioned this physical expression of hers, though she noted the marks occasionally. In mythology, lovers who had been apart for extended periods used this to show intense affection. The "scathing" was used to give proof of the female's possession of the man. I could feel a form of dominance being exerted by Mirabella. She may have expressed some superiority, but I did not care.

I wanted more.

Mirabella

I thought, "Okay, Aspen was one thing. It was remote, and now I have him in my city.

What was I thinking?"

It would be easy keeping busy here, Broadway, and then running around town till he dropped would work. My needs were growing, and more than one man had bolted from my lair. This was different; I vaguely remember that something unique, biological, smell, taste, and touch brought him alive in Aspen.

It was simple: I gave to get.

No one alive but my mother knows my secret. No one.

I must ask, "Did he remember? Did he know?

The taste of him makes me half crazy.

No one alive knows the secret. No one.

Does he know?

Does he remember?

It was 25 years ago, but it is still "vivid" to me.

My thoughts are running all over the map.

I had a time of youth when I may have been intemperate. Zach's taste reminded me why I was attracted to him but simultaneously fearful. He possessed something I had not had since we began.

SUBWAY

Saturday came quickly, and the quest continued.

Mirabella issued a challenge.

'I bet you will not ride the subway."

"Why?" I asked.

"You will not want to," Mirabella said.

"Bullshit," I replied. "I used to ride the subway every day."

"Let's take the subway to the One World Trade," she offered.

"Sure, why not?"

"I did not think you would take the train anymore."

"What are you thinking, girl." "Unusual observation," I thought.

When we met 25 years ago, the train was always the traveling venue to our destinations. Often the ride was as exciting and interesting as our destination. Now that we were older, the sight of others, younger others, brought back memories. We found ourselves looking at each other smiling in remembrance.

Since it was Saturday, the traffic on the train was sparse. COVID has dissuaded people from wanting to be in close contact with others.

We were at the One World Trade Center in 10 minutes, and it was a hoot watching Mirabella watch me.

The contact with people on the subway is exemplified by the rich, the poor, and the people you may never meet in any other way. New Yorkers still ride the subway. It is part of the culture; you see humanity in all its forms.

The Subway is Manhattan style. The subway is a public system that has existed for years. There are 472 stations, and they connect nearly everywhere in the city. The cool part is that the system has run 24/7 forever. At least 6 million people must use this thing daily, about 2 billion rides per year.

I wondered at the expense of this "public conveyance." The New York Subway System was vastly different from the public transportation systems I had experienced in Europe. After World War Two, Europe was forced to rebuild from the ground up. Most countries took the opportunity to embrace modernity and planning. Today's European transportation systems were bright, clean, timely, and reliable.

The New York Subway system is more like an aging dancer. A bit rough around the edges, seen better days, and cantankerous. The smell of the subway is a combination of a hundred years of weather, billions of feet, foods, and mold. There is nothing elegant about the subway, but like the dancer, it has seen it all.

Chapter XV

EATALY

"Since we're at One World Trade, why don't we eat lunch here?" Mirabella suggested. "There is this fantastic place near my office for lunch. They import most things daily from Italy."

"I didn't know you had an office in One World Trade," I said. "That has to be an interesting story."

"Maybe we'll talk about it one day, but let's get lunch for now."

Eataly NYC is an excellent concept of multiple restaurants in a single building. Their flagship store is the Flatiron store. World Trade Center Tower's Eataly has five different Italian restaurants for us to choose from. Since we weren't terribly hungry, we decided on "Vino and …" a fantastic restaurant that seemed to occupy an entire floor. We grabbed a quick lunch at one of Mirabelle's favorite spots. Mirabelle has been obsessed with Agnolotti, a form of pasta since childhood. The very adult version here comes with roasted veal, sausage, escarole, and Parmigianino Reggiano, and she nearly swoons over the dish. My Tagliatelle Bolognese is sublime.

In addition to the restaurant, there was an Italian market where I had the opportunity to learn about the many cuisines of Italy. The elegant décor and variety of small plates fit our needs perfectly.

The wine and view made the entire moment seem suspended in time.

As we ate, the entire area of the former World Trade Center came alive. After lunch, we briefly toured the 9/11 Memorial and reflected on all the changes in Manhattan over the past few years.

Mirabella asked, "Do you remember when we had lunch at Windows of the World.?

"Of course," I replied.

Windows on the World

It seemed like only a few days ago that Mirabella and I had lunch at the then World Trade Center. The reputation of "The Greatest Bar on Earth" was accurate. The restaurant was large, with what seemed like 40000+ square feet, and was located at the top of the North Tower.

We were young, and this place seemed terrific. They had a dress code, which was strictly enforced for men. Jackets were required. New York kept higher standards at that time. Looking out from the bar through the full-length windows, you could see where the Hudson and East Rivers meet. I was showing off when I invited Mirabella to Windows on the World.

At the time, our relationship seemed to be going very well. We were not living together, but we spent at least two nights a week together. With the odd lunch and dinner meet ups we spent a lot of time together. I was seriously thinking of asking her to make it a more formal agreement. I hadn't looked at rings, but I did get a second key to my apartment. I still had a couple of years to go until I received my inheritance, so there was time. My job was going well and I looked forward to meeting all of the terms and conditions that the inheritance required.

I hadn't said anything to Mirabella yet, doing the typical guy thing of surprising her. But today was a good time to offer her the key to my apartment. We were at the nicest restaurant I could think of, and afford, with the greatest woman I knew. When would be better?

With the restaurant found on the 106th and 107th floors of the building, jets could regularly be seen flying beneath your view of the New York harbor and the Statue of Liberty. Wandering around the restaurant was encouraged to view the harbor, the Hudson and East Rivers, and the North view of the city. The city was as much a part of the restaurant as the staff and the food. A New York Times food critic once said that nobody will ever go to the Windows on the World to eat, but even a food person can now be content dining at the Windows of the World. The view of the city was the main course.

The food and wine landscape were undergoing a revolution as the gold-standard French cuisine of earlier decades was replaced with invention, creativity, fresh ingredients, and a uniquely American attitude. Leaders such as the French Laundry and Chateau Montelena appeared on the international stage to prove that American cuisine had arrived.

"I remember we had a wonderful lunch, tasty wine, and enjoyed the view. I was captivated by you then. You were gorgeous and vivacious, and I wanted to be with you. Then you told me our relationship was over. When you walked out and left me at the table that way, I was shattered. I took a flight to Denver and on to Vail. After several days of drinking to excess, I asked a girl to marry me. Luckily, she said "no," and I started to rebuild my emotional life."

I'm sorry," said Mirabella. "It just wasn't the right time for me. I tried to explain it to you at the time."

I remembered the time sadly as if it were from an earlier, simpler time, which it was. It is hard to imagine a single event changing the course of a country and a lifetime more profoundly than 9-11. Like the rest of the country, I was appalled, outraged, angry, and vengeful. It seems like a distant scene in a book that is not very good.

Windows on the World was an eclectic mix of restaurants and bars overlooking New York. As we waited, a liveried man arrived and introduced himself as KZ. We soon found that "KZ" was Kevin Zraly, the world-renowned Sommelier for the Windows on the World. He quizzed us on our dining choices and tastes, then offered us a selection of wines for our enjoyment. We chose a red and a white of his suggestion. Our dinner at the Window of the World was exceptional in its ambiance and service. Our food was a dish of oysters and clams of local origin. The food was excellent, and her dish was poached chicken and saffron. I enjoyed a crispy duck with three purees.

The wine was from California, and a better Cabernet was never served. Mirabella enjoyed her Chardonnay but did not feel it was anything special. KZ immediately replaced it with something more to her liking. Napa had only a few hundred vineyards at the time, and our wine sommelier had made the choice.

Such times are hard to forget, as Mirabella was an elegant and beautiful companion.

"I know," I said. "I guess I needed to go through the storm then to see the rainbow." I smiled at her.

I remembered the time sadly as if it were from an earlier, simpler time, which it was. It is hard to imagine a single event changing the course of a country and a lifetime more profoundly than 9-11. Like the rest of the country, I was appalled, outraged, angry, and vengeful. It seems like a distant scene in a book that is not very good.

We Ubered to Grand Central station so I could take a train to Westchester. We could have just grabbed a subway and headed there, but Grand Central holds memories for me, and I wanted to visit again. The sight of the building's interior from the front door is little to equal.

As we walked past the Vanderbilt Avenue entrance to Grand Central Terminal, we realized we had missed lunch and would likely be close to hangry if we tried to wait until dinner. We stopped at The Campbell and ordered lobster rolls and chocolate chip cookies to share. Hopefully, the double espressos will keep us going until the rest of our "to-do" list is completed today.

The restaurant that defines Grand Central is The Campbell. The restaurant where a million or more business deals have happened is within the walls of The Campbell. With a history that includes being a railroad jail and several renovations costing millions, the Campell Bar defines Grand Central Station. Millions of business deals and many affairs started and ended at the Campell. The Campbell is also where all the commuters of a certain status met before the sojourn to the suburbs. The number of affairs that started and ended at the Campbell are beyond number. I wondered what movement and action drives people to do things "sometimes" not in their best interest. People from all places stopped for "cocktails" and a quick meeting. Mirabella talked about her time waiting for trains to her home in the upstate. At one time, she made the trek several times a week. The cocktail she preferred was a "Manhattan."

Mirabella said, "All trains lead to Grand Central."

One of the landmark icons of Grand Central is the four-faced opal clock in the Main Concourse. "Meet me at the clock" is a catchphrase for New Yorkers. And one of my fondest memories occurred in Grand Central. Christmas Eve, 1999.

My soon-to-be wife and I were returning from Westchester to Scarsdale. We were going to stay with her father and needed to change trains.

The feeling on the train that evening showed the heart of New York. Kids were playing in the aisle as kids should, and my soul felt the warmth of one little stand-out boy; his father was sitting. You're not on the train for fun or if you have a lot of money, and here we all were, but the peace of that evening sated my soul for a memorable holiday moment. The subway is the way all true New Yorkers move around town.

This little boy approached me and stood there, swaying in the aisle. He looked from Leigh to me and back again. Then he smiled, reached out both hands and touched us on the knees. A sharp shock ran through my body, and I could see Leigh react. I was suddenly engulfed in warmth and peacefulness that was out of context with our current situation. I looked at Leigh, and an almost palpable wave of love and emotion flowed between us. When I looked back, the little boy was gone. I saw him sitting on his father's lap, and they got off at the next stop.

Our weekend ended, and Mirabella asked the famous question once again?

"The time is going too fast. Why don't you come back Friday afternoon?" she asked.

I was dumbfounded for the second time.

"Count on it."

I was starting to understand how Mirabella made decisions. She knew somehow that I could move things quickly to suit her. As we sipped our coffee, we continued our back-and-forth conversation. Just two more travelers leaving their footprints in the sands of time.

Nature?

My trip back to the mountain was uneventful, but the promise and excitement of Mirabella was growing and needed. I craved being with her again. I worked all week with a distracted impatience that Rachel noticed at once.

"What is wrong with you, Mr. Zach?" she asked. "You are biting everyone's head off for no reason. Are you feeling okay?"

"I'm sorry, Rachel," I said. "I just have a lot on my mind. Yes, I feel fine. I'll try to be a little more civil."

With Rachel's words in my mind, I continued through the week. In addition to the standard work-related issues, I attended two charity functions, one in Charlotte and one in Asheville. I left substantial checks with each group and felt fulfilled that I had helped others.

Friday came, and off to Manhattan. I traveled back to New York.

We met at Mirabella's apartment. She always had a surprise. The weekends during the plague were limited to a small sample of what Manhattan had to offer. Mirabella said we were going to a type of event that had permeated during the age of COVID-19.

"There is an exhibit I think you will like; you up for an adventure?

POP UP Weekend

Sistine Chapel

Saturday morning in Manhattan. The city's energy was slowly coming alive, and we were back on the train again. We visited a pop-up presenting the Sistine Chapel paintings on our next venture. These appeared to be life-size. The pop-up was in SoHo.

Michelangelo painted the ceiling of the Sistine Chapel in the 1500s. His fame lies predominately in the frescoes that decorate the interior of the Chapel. The artwork moves you emotionally, spiritually, and mystically. I noticed nine pictures that depicted Creation, Man, and the Fall from God's Grace. Michelangelo painted the ceiling, and the effort changed the course of art. The belief is that this ceiling is one of man's most outstanding artistic achievements.

The pop-up was made of life-size prints of the frescoes. The experience enthralled Mirabella. It seemed she had visited the Sistine Chapel, had an eerie knowledge of the painting, and had a personal experience with it. At first, I thought Mirabella was continuing her fascination with museums, but this was more.

Her family was Italian and that fit, but she seemed much more interested than a casual obsession. It appeared from our banter that she was there during the painting by Michelangelo. How could this be possible? I chalked off exaggeration, but something lingered. It merged with the vagrant thought from Aspen, growing in importance but not yet complete. Mirabella seemed to be from a unique lineage. Her actions were sometimes inconsistent with her seemingly intimate knowledge of Rome. Her earlier family lineage was from Hungry when the Romans ruled. She spoke of her parents serving Roman households and dying in an attack by the Visigoths. She spoke meaningfully about her years as an orphan and how she made her way to Rome to meet Michaelangelo and Raphael.

Mirabella seemed to transcend time; once again, a trance-like state occupied her voice and demeanor as she stared at the pictures. The pop-up showed Stories of the Bible via the frescoes. The story of Jesus from the Catholic perspective is overwhelming.

Mirabella shared that when she was in Rome, the Sistine Chapel was covered with the residue of the water that seeped through the roof. The frescoes were eventually restored; however, the stories they could tell. How many brilliant and calculating people have seen the work of Michelangelo?

I listened to Mirabella with a skeptical ear. How could this fifty-something woman have been in the Sistine Chapel then? How could she have been an Orphan when her mother called her in Aspen? That would make her over 500 years old. Impossible! But that little part of my brain whispered, "no, it's not."

GOD

There is a fresco in the Sistine Chapel that depicts God and Adam. I had seen pictures many times but never seen the fresco in person. It started me thinking of man trying to equate something like the infinite into an anthropomorphic image for those of the time to relate to their lives.

When I say I saw God, I see the most outstanding picture I have ever seen that shows God as a human. The painting by Michelangelo gave a human look to a divine entity. He was depicted as a significantly older man with plenty of flesh in the frescos. He reaches out to Adam, leaving a small gap between their fingers, signifying the unfinished work of man and his place as a creation of the almighty.

The exhibit was a fantastic way to start a Saturday morning in Manhattan.

Time alone was now the primary focus of our budding renewed relationship. The sight and vision of Mirabella were an aphrodisiac to me. Before we left the exhibit, there was a revelation.

Mirabella grew "Wings" by standing in front of the exhibition poster. We laughed at the frivolity of the sight, and then I took her place. Pictures all around.

Mirabella said, "Time for coffee." We reached the closest Coffee House, and with the weather perfect, we sat on the street sipping and noshing.

Somehow, our time passed so fast that a day would seem like an hour. As we kept talking, it seemed we needed more time. We would have time to visit, talk, remember, and look forward to new adventures. Aspen had been the start of this new relationship. Manhattan was even better.

The idea of revisiting the past places of our youth was exhilarating. We discussed how we once frequented the Village and Soho and decided on the upcoming weekends to "explore" those places again. We discussed how we once frequented the Village and Soho and agreed that we would "explore" those places again on the upcoming weekends. The day ended, and the evening became more intense. I felt like a young man embarking on my first relationship.

It struck me that Mirabella was committing to future weekends together. I stirred my coffee and luxuriated in anticipation of those weekends. I fantasized about the things we'd do together. The little voice in the back of my head was now mumbling to me. I couldn't make it out, but it was growing.

Mirabella wanted to show me some of the more touristy parts of town. Several reviews from Zagat's pushed her recommendations, and traveling around Manhattan on the weekend is easy.

THE SEAPORT

During our storming of Manhattan, we went to the Seaport several times. I had once worked on Wall Street, and the Seaport became a significant attraction with some of the finest seafood in the city. I then lived in Brooklyn Heights for a time, and the trip over the Brooklyn Bridge and the never-quiet Brooklyn Queens Expressway were part of my life. Mirabella and I also recalled having drinks at Harry's back in the day when we were publishing neophytes. Today, we arrived a little early for our reservation and offered to wait in the bar, but a table was quickly made available. We nibble on a shared Greek salad as we anticipate the excellent entrees: grilled salmon for Mirabelle and the house specialty, Beef Wellington, for me. The entrees arrive perfectly executed, including service of the beef from the cart and the salmon grilled to a medium rare with an accompaniment of bearnaise sauce. It's a variation from the menu offering truffle sauce, but Mirabelle was "put off" years ago by truffles and prefers lemon and tarragon with salmon. I've always been convinced there's a separate compartment of our digestive system reserved for desserts, and this meal bears that out. Neither of us could finish our entrees or the side of creamed spinach, but we shared the chocolate layer cake down to the last crumb.

Mirabella

So far so good! I've walked him nearly into the ground and he is still standing. Clearly, he hasn't succumbed to the sloth and obesity of the average American male. That bodes well for my needs later tonight.

Zach has become a marvelous storyteller. He has regaled me with stories of the past 25 years we have been apart. He is both funny and serious at turns. I can tell he misses his wife. Her death was obviously hard on him. But he has moved well beyond the grieving process. I find myself seriously attracted to him again. I'll need to monitor my feelings.

I still remember how hard it was to choose between Zach and Jacob. Ultimately, I chose Jacob because I felt My profile to the world would be lower. Little did I know that he and I would end up so successful together.

Tonight will be the next test. Can I get what I need from Zach without harming him in the process? Can I restrain my passions and my secrets without him noticing? He's leaving tomorrow so I'll have some time to think.

Chapter XVI

I flew home from Westchester, as had become my habit. Mirabella scolded me about using a private jet for my trips. I reminded her that our Special Presidential Envoy for Climate owned three private jets and traveled on private military transport worldwide. My journey from Charlotte to Westchester once a week could hardly compare.

As the week progressed, I came down off the emotional and physical high of being with Mirabella. My thinking became more precise, and trivial things Mirabella said and did during our time together started to pop up in my head. There were beginning to be too many inconsistencies in Mirabella's narrative. Maybe she was joking about being with Michaelangelo and Raphael, maybe not. I am uncertain. But her pull on me is strong enough that I will ride this train to the last station just to be with her. If she is over 500 years old, I want to know her secret so we can spend the next 500 years together. Yeah, I have it bad.

My business partners and compatriots noticed the difference in me. Some commented, and some merely watched me out of the side of their eyes. Rachel asked me some version of "Who is she? Nearly every day. I think it had become a puzzle for her to solve.

Elizabeth, on the other hand, was far less circumspect.

"So, Dad, who are you seeing in New York?" she asked one morning at breakfast. Her pregnancy is barely noticeable, but the flush in her cheeks is pronounced.

"What makes you think I'm seeing someone in New York?"

"Cut the crap, Dad. You keep going up there for the weekend. I doubt you are wandering around town by yourself. Who is she?"

I stared at her for a minute, trying to decide my response. Finally, I said, "She's an old friend from my publishing days. Her husband recently died, and she reached out to me on the Internet."

"I'm happy for your Dad. It's well past time for you to move on from Mom. You'll never forget or replace her, but you deserve happiness. What's her name?"

We talked for another hour about Mirabella and our meetups. Elizabeth was enthusiastic about the relationship, but I cautioned her to remain calm.

"I don't know where we are going with this. She may decide it's over anytime, and I would never see her again. She did exactly that 25 years ago. She invited me to lunch at Windows on the World, then dumped me like a bag of trash off the back of an old ship. Just be cool, and let's see where it leads."

"If she treated you like that 25 years ago, why would you want to rekindle the relationship?"

"There is something about her that is almost a physical addiction. I can't explain it. I know I need to have it."

She nodded and agreed, but I could tell she wouldn't let this go. Like a dog with a bone, she would worry it to death until she met Mirabella, something that would not happen soon. The voice in my head was getting louder, but I still couldn't make out what it was saying.

I left for Westchester on Friday afternoon.

We started the weekend in the financial district. It had been an earlier haunt of ours.

Harry's

This place was a watering hole for the people of Wall Street for generations. It has a dress code, and wow, how that made things feel more like my New York. The wine list and the suede. booths make for a great afternoon. The bar and the pub room are great ways to celebrate a classic martini. Mirabella looked as if I remembered her from long ago. Her style and flair were uniquely cosmopolitan.

The Seaport area of the financial district was not a force 25 years before but now was a dominant scene to the day-to-day Wall Street worker. The restaurants and the festive air of people enjoying themselves for the afternoon are uniquely New York.

I was quick to notice the aroma of marijuana. Legalization was underway in the state, but I gather the NYPD was letting things ride. Usually, when I was in Colorado, the aroma would be around occasionally, but here, the intense aroma was a bit overwhelming.

The Fulton

The waiter's introduction into Mirabella's world was seamless. He was from the Midwest, somewhere in Iowa. He was ecstatic to be in New York and had the hubris of youth to propel him onto the scene. He wanted to be an actor and was working to support his passion. With his first name, Billy, where else could he be from? Mirabella continued with her engagement of the waiter. What part of Iowa are you from? Her banter was taking a turn I had seen starting in Aspen. Billy was putty in her hands and ended up telling her his whole life story, including the story of the girl he left behind. The funny thing was she did it without effort.

Our favorite restaurant quickly became the Fulton in the Tin Building, a part of the old Fish Market. The Seaport area had a connection to Mirabella. A family member often brought her to the location, and she inferred from this that her family had arrived in the United States before Ellis Island was a destination for immigrants. The little voice in my head was getting louder.

One notable feature of Fulton's interior is a unique mural of an underwater scene on the wall. The almost dreamlike painting had to be painted by hand. The suggestion it gave me was deep involvement with the sea's mysteries. With crabs, squid, coral, and other denizens of the deep, the mural provided a tranquil distraction while waiting for your meal. Another outstanding visual element of Fulton's is the breathtaking view of the Brooklyn Bridge just outside the windows. The menu is a kaleidoscope of breakfast, lunch, and dinner-like items, and we home in on what feels like "brunch." Mirabella's avocado toast with smoked salmon and a perfectly poached egg fits the bill and wins rave reviews. I go with the entirely decadent fried oysters benedict with a "dusting" of Old Bay and find myself wishing for more than a mere dusting of the spicy seasoning.

This restaurant has a great indoor and outdoor arrangement for seating at the confluence of Fulton Street and the East River. The seaport area had pristine weather, and we sat outside to enjoy the fall. A unique thing was happening all over New York, and that issue was the usage of marijuana. Mirabella was not a fan of cannabis; she had mentioned it several times. Zach believed differently but had no dream of rocking the boat on that one. The smell in any public gathering was pronounced and gave more of a Colorado vibe. We ate dinner in the Fulton restaurant, which produces some of the world's most fantastic fish dishes. To quote Mirabella, "Food- Pricy and divine."

Mirabella has that unique New York-Manhattan attitude. You see it with her walk and the attitude of her bag perched perfectly on her shoulders. It was something to see twenty years ago. Manhattan held many memories of our time together—the places we frequented and the seeming intrigue she could have over Zach's memories.

The Village

During our earlier time together, we often went to Greenwich Village. Mirabella, in her playful mood, reminded me. "You know I'm younger than you."

Well, yes, that is plain. I wonder if she was "legal" when we first met. Given our time together, I did not even know her age when she liked to dance all evening. Mirabella and I would frequent a local place in the village in our early days. It was near NYU, an area full of students, artists, and actors. The neighborhood on the west side of lower Manhattan has two identifiable roads "Broadway and Houston Street.

My fascination with the village began when I was a child. I heard about the Village as an artist's center, a bohemian capital, and home of the Beat Generation.

Mirabella asked, "Do you remember when we used to go to the Knickerbocker?"

It all came back to me quickly:

The Knickerbocker was where we would have a beer and meet her friends. The food had reasonable prices and huge portions; two things going for it.

When we went in, we noticed that many celebrities frequented this bar. We were shopping for stars, as we were informed by the waiter that Chris Noth, Alec Baldwin, Susan Sarandon, and many other notable stars were all regulars.

I'm told Harry Connick got his start there, but maybe it's a myth.

The bar has wood-paneled walls and turn-of-the-century posters. The feeling of old New York comes alive when you are in a large leather booth and the brass rails accentuating the marble bar.

Our waiter, Claude, mentioned that Charles Lindbergh supposedly signed his agreement to fly nonstop over the Atlantic in the room where we sat.

The Sullivan Street Theater.

Some light years before, we went to this Soho Institution. The play we saw was "Fantasticks." The story, an allegory, centers around two fathers who trick their children into falling in love. The fathers set up obstacles for them to keep overcoming. There is seasonal nostalgia to the song "Try to Remember." It was said when the show closed 40-50 years later, showing the dramatic force of this intimate show. The set transforms through music into a rich and human story of memory. Mirabella reminded me that we went there due to a lack of funds. I agreed she was probably right.

I then reminded her she "stood me up" once years ago. I had great seats for a real Broadway Musical. I saved my money for weeks to get two tickets to "Cabaret." I invited her to the show. When it came time to meet, she never showed up.

"Yes, I know," she said, "that was the week I met Jakob. I was so over the moon that I couldn't remember my name, much less a date with you. I am sorry."

"That's okay," I said. "I ended up selling the tickets to a couple looking for last-minute tickets. That was the evening I became a scalper."

Mirabella laughed and tossed back her drink.

"All's well that ends well," she said.

The Soho area was known as an area of Artists when we were dating. Many of the buildings had been commercial lofts, which provided large and unobstructed spaces and were needed for natural sunlight. Many artists lived in the rooms.

Most of these spaces were also used illegally as living spaces despite being neither zoned nor equipped for residential use. This widespread zoning violation was ignored for decades, as the artist-occupants used the space for no commercial use. This changed in the 70s as New York grew.

Mirabella, the New Yorker, suggested we closely examine the cast-iron architecture in Soho.

Mirabella:

The New York weekends were moving differently from my original thoughts. The upcoming events at the Met would help define where this was going. If only temporarily, this was not a terrible thing. The secrets of my life and family legacy were to be something to deal with, but not now. *Zach seemed to be reliving some of his past through our adventures, and while interesting. I've been here before. It's a bit of a re-run. Most of my life had been spent moving and focusing on the moment. Things were changing due to other issues that would soon arise.*

We went to Soho.

We went to the Village.

I think Zach may have been recreating a particular fantasy. With only a few weeks left in my plan, this would work.

Back in Mirabella's apartment, the discussion went to our private life. How could we start spending this much time together and have it be this effortless?

Mirabella was becoming a little tired of being my Manhattan tour guide; as she said, she was feeling a little weary of returning to the routine here in the city.

"Should we meet in Colorado?" "Have I been neglecting my new house and my boys?" asked Mirabella.

"If Colorado is the place, I'm all for it," I said. "May I give you another suggestion?"

Mirabella said sure, "It would be a short weekend in Colorado. Travel is still a pain."

"You mentioned you loved your short trip to Montreal. Canada opened up last week. How about we head to Montreal, then over to Quebec? It would be a shorter trip and allow you to return to Manhattan on Sunday evening. Why don't we head to Canada for the weekend as a palate cleanser?" These surprises kept our world intriguing.

"This will be an adventure," she said. "The French have a unique way of looking at the world."

Taking her smile to mean yes, I, without any compunction, made the reservations. I was not completely honest. While Montreal would have met Mirabella's need for museums, I thought the trip might be my only chance to get Mirabella to Quebec City. The weekend ended with what was becoming familiar and inviting. How bizarre that two almost strangers are so comfortable with each other? I caught the train to Westchester, made my trip back to Westchester, and flew back to my mountain airstrip.

My trip home was dominated by my thoughts and memories of the weekend. The little voice in my head was growing louder. I couldn't understand what it was saying yet, but I knew it was about Mirabella. Our time together was nearly magical. The world took on an extra sharp tinge. Colors were deeper, laughter easier, our physical joining's immeasurable. But three days after leaving her presence, things returned to "normal." My reactions became short and snarky. My senior managers often remarked that I'd gotten up on the wrong side of the bed. I found myself cancelling Wednesday meetings and taking the day to recover from my weekend.

Sarah and Elizabeth both noticed the change. Elizabeth even commented on it during lunch one day.

"I don't know what's going on sweetie," I told her. "When I'm with Mirabella, the world is a better place. I feel better, I'm sharper and more present in life. When I come home, I slowly drag down into what I now call the "new normal." It's almost as if she has an addictive effect on me."

"Sounds like love to me, Dad."

"It may be. But I remember the last time I felt these feelings towards her. She walked away and married another guy. Then I met your mom. Now they are both gone and the path is clear for us if we want it. I'm just in the once bitten twice shy zone."

"Well, Dad, you have a choice. You can live in the past and worry if she's going to dump you. Or you can live for the moment and enjoy the time you two have together. Let the future work itself out on its own. I think you should go with the flow and see what comes up."

Chapter XVII

Montreal

Mirabella had a favorite museum in Montreal, and I had a surprise that I would spring on her once we landed. We made the plans and counted the days. Friday afternoon, we boarded Air Canada for Montreal.

Entrance into Canada.

Arrival is always enjoyable when you go to Canada. The Canadian border and customs personnel are a focused group of professionals. Even if they detain you for hours, they do it with courtesy and civilization. The Sûreté du Québec has overriding powers of discretion, like the local police in the US. Upon arrival, Mirabella and I had to go through customs, and the most repeated question was, "Are you here on business," they are very formal.

Regardless, we cleared customs without undue delay and headed for the rental car terminal, which was directly across the roadway from the Terminal. I reserved a full-sized car for us with respect to the Avis team in Denver. Mirabella took the passenger side and immediately commandeered the radio. Soon, familiar melodies sung in French filled the interior. To my surprise, Mirabella began to sing along.

"I never knew you spoke French," I said.

"I am a woman of many mysteries."

We careened down the road listening to French Rock and roll.

The Hotel Bonaventure

We arrived in Canada, and the winds of Autumn were upon us. We drove to our first hotel of the trip, where we would stay in a unique hotel chosen purposely for its proximity to the train station.

The Hotel Bonaventure of Montreal is connected to the Metro station and all the commuter trains. The hotel is large enough that it has its own postal code. The building is a combination of modern style and historic architecture. Beautiful gardens accentuate the pathways between wings and rooms. A year-round pool caters to the cold hardy. There are impressively decorated nooks and crannies scattered throughout the hotel to cater to a visitor's every whim. I was sure that Mirabella would enjoy our stay. Mirabella sensed something was "going on" when, upon arrival, the desk clerk confirmed our reservations and the arrangements I made with them on the phone to travel to Quebec by train. With a side look and a questioning raise of her eyebrows, Mirabella nodded to herself and remained quiet as we checked in.

It was cold and dreary outside, and we decided to stay close to the hotel for convenience. The day of travel tired us out and being in the comfortable confines of the Bonaventure was a godsend. After having drinks in the bar, we found an excellent restaurant located in the Hotel. The menu was a surprise. It was diverse, and they offered an Ossa Bucco and a beef shoulder. It was a chilly night, and the comfort food was inviting.

I surprised Mirabella with an impromptu trip to Quebec City the following day. Quebec City is the most romantic city in the Northern Hemisphere and the only walled city north of Mexico. Founded in 1608,

Quebec has been the site of more than half a dozen battles in the 17th and 18th centuries as France and England fought for dominance. Stepping into the walled city is a trip to Europe hundreds of years ago with all the modern conveniences.

We had breakfast from room service, and the train station was nearly at the hotel's front door. Mirabella had relaxed into the "changing plans" that I presented. The train ride is about 3 hours, and we chose to take advantage of the first-class fare. Honestly, it was only incrementally more in price but offered champagne. We enjoyed our champagne as the plains and rivers passed by our window. We chatted and passed the time enjoyably.

Gare centrale de Montreal

The station was somewhat of an antithesis of Grand Central. It was clean and had a little Art Deco bas-relief frieze on the interior. Much more utilitarian than visual. The art broke up the blandness of the walls and presented vignettes of Canadian sports, work, and life. We quickly made our way through the station and settled into our seats.

Montreal was established 34 years after Quebec. Nearly 450 years after its inception, Mirabella and I would explore the old part of Quebec, relishing its historic charm and walking the cobblestone streets. We planned to visit the Chateau Frontenac, enjoy French-inspired cuisines, and walk along the Dufferin Boardwalk to view the St. Lawrence River. We hoped to be treated to up-close views of giant ore ships traveling the water.

Through family history, I was aware of the close connection of the people of the international Appalachian mountain chain. The French settled into the territory at the same time as the Lord Proprietors in the English areas of North America. Family traditions going back 400 years are a mainstay of the stability of the founders.

Mirabella was interested in the history of Quebec. As we traveled, she told me a story of dark times for females during the Salem witchcraft trials were occurring. Canada became a refuge for women under attack. She also mentioned that women's movements of the 19th century included campaigns of pacifism, temperance, and labor and rights for women. Before that, in the 1600s, the world was less civilized. The Protestant work ethic was a controlling feature of the New World. France had set up Catholic outposts in many areas. She spoke of the communes as before, with almost an intimate knowledge of them. Her comments revolved around outcast women who formed outposts as havens from persecution. As we rode, she asked a question from out of nowhere.

"Do you know the word Grimoire?"

"Can't say that I do. Never heard of it."

Grimoire

Then the Grimoire arrived in our world. Mirabella explained it is a plain and straightforward book that never draws attention to itself. The Grimoire is a general name given to various texts setting out the names of demons and instructions on how to raise them. Effectively, a grimoire is a book of black magic in which a wizard relies for all the necessary advice and instruction on raising spirits and casting spells.

The story that Mirabella shared was from a different place and time. Anyone owning the book would have been burned at the stake.

The Salem witch trials appeared to be more than just religious terror but a living, breathing fear that was still alive. Mirabella explained that early communities often sought certain women for medical help when the communes were set up. The ladies of the communes saw the Grimoire as a recipe manual. However, it was much more. Mirabella spoke with an assured knowledge of the Grimoire and its uses. She also told of the penalties for being caught with the book. Then she said casually:

"I have a copy that is over 300 years old."

I was fascinated but somewhat appalled at the details she shared. The little voice in my head grew louder again but was still indistinct. There was some connection between Mirabella and the details she was sharing. I felt I was nearly at the point of understanding.

Our train pulled into Quebec on time. The Quebec station is called Gare du Palais." Where the Montreal station was small and straightforward, the Gare du Palais in Quebec is more like New York's Central Station. A vast main hall reminiscent of many European churches dominates the building. Outside, the station looks like a modernist Brunelleschi designed the space.

The door of the Chateau Frontenac is only steps away from the train station. The hotel made recommendations for a great afternoon of taste. The hotel concierge suggested we try the Champlain Restaurant for lunch. He said we would love the cuisine with a touch of new French bistro flavors.

The villages of Quebec were all around as we spent the next few hours conversing with a couple from Montreal on a weekend getaway. Je Me Souviens- "I remember" was part of the inherent meaning of Quebec. A fellow traveler shared that the providences grow with a quote.

"I remember that I was born under the lily. I grow under the rose." A reference to the mixed French/English history of the area. There is a vicarious nostalgia for all that is food in Quebec.

We chose to eat at the Champlain Restaurant. The elegant and minimalist fare suited our need for tasty food and a place to escape the wind. I arranged for them to open early and serve us as a private party. They would open to the public at 6:00 p.m. Mirabella chose the Discovery Menu: foie gras, Arctic Char, cranberry kombucha, and black forest cake. I chose the Signature Menu: foie gras, duck, and apple compote. We decided on a lovely Chardonnay from Chateau Montelena.

Mirabella

My first foray into sharing my secrets with Zach went well. He was fascinated and appalled by the Grimoire and my descriptions of the book. Most people are. But to his credit, I sensed no revulsion or disapproval. In our previous time together, I never moved this far with him. If I had, I might not have been able to marry Jacob. Did I miss an opportunity? Or did I just postpone another great love of my life? Only time will tell, but I am getting worried about how far and how fast we are moving.

QUEBEC CITY

We walked lunch off exploring Quebec City in the mid-afternoon. The St. Lawrence River looked forbiddingly cold. Slowly, we walked back to the hotel with the wind reminding us that fall had arrived. We walked along the old city's walls, checking out the famous ramparts. Further strolling took us to Petit Champlain, a fantastic street filled with shops and art galleries.

Canadian Octobers make one glad to be alive. The vision of red from beech, birch, and maple trees adds to the city's atmosphere. Transition time narrows the window between summer's vibrancy and winter's starkness. For us, it is perfection as no crowds exist, and we received the best of the city. It has a romantic charm and brings Paris to you. You find yourself in a better mood.

First was the need for a great afternoon auberge/café, this time the Battuto restaurant. The Waiters and wine purveyors were storytellers- The description of the food for each dish was insightful and meaningful. The people seemed to work well together.

For dinner, we chose Buvette Scott. We were told that the specialty is local fare with a menu that changes often. The best part of the experience was the wine list.

Quebec City seems to be a city where all people are from elsewhere. It has almost a Parisian feel with the mix of cultures.

Chateau Frontenac

The imposing structure of the Chateau is a powerful attribute of the city. The Château Frontenac makes one feel as if in a castle. It becomes an eccentric and colorful world.

138

1 Rue des Carrières, Québec (ville), CA G1R 5J5

I rented a small suite as it fit Mirabella and my style of having private space.

After dinner, we toured the walled city and wandered the Quartier Petit Champlain. The rumor is that in the 1600s, three Catholic sisters traveled to Quebec to open a hospital and monastery. The purpose was to heal the body, soul, and mind. It is still working. It seemed to be in the best of the heart of Paris. Quebec City is a place that may want to be your lover. The city has a style and panache that seems to create a "hush" of respect for the town. It is calming to be in the charm of Quebec City.

Winding around the corner was a jazz club in the Hotel Clarendon; it was a small venue, but it was quintessentially appropriate for the moment in other parts of the world. Walking around the corner and seeing a smoky jazz bar was an experience. Suddenly, you find yourself in a new world that has a bit of being cosmopolitan but at the same time more essential than the one we live in.

As we walked down the old streets Mirabella suddenly stopped and tilted her head to the side. I stood beside her and waited as she appeared to be listening to something only she could hear. I waited a few minutes and softly said, "are you all right?"

It was as if I had woken Sleeping Beauty from her slumber. Her eyes refocused and she seemed to return to the present. She laughed it off, but a strange shadow lurked in her eyes as we walked on. A shadow I've never seen in her before.

The Clarendon

It's an old haunt of mine. The Clarendon Hotel has a unique jazz bar, "Mothers," in the heart of Old Quebec. Think about the Peter Gunn series from 1960. Finding this gem during the pandemic was a lifesaver. It is that cool.

The hotel is a historical reference that dates to the 1600s. It was a possible connection to the Lord proprietors when I first found the hotel some 22 years before, and my memories were of a delightful evening with a girl named Rosalind. Rosalind was my rebound relationship after Mirabella dumped me the first time. We spent three months in a high-octane, high-risk, affaire houleuse. People were smoking, and it reminded me of when Bars were filled with smoke and the sounds of jazz. The mood was perfect for being in another world.

After spending the evening together, we went back to the Chateau. The front looks like a European castle, but the inside is state-of-the-art.

Stepping into the hotel is like walking into a world of luxury and beauty. Marble and wood paneling set the décor, and small nooks for reading or business meetings dot the first floor. Brass-trimmed tables dot the well-equipped bar. The rooms are well-lit and spacious.

We settled into our room and opened a bottle of wine. We became amazingly comfortable in an unusual way. Mirabella had a flair and style that was a fantastic, alluring vision. Her face seemed more chiseled, highlighted, with a touch of feral. It was a look I had not seen, and it surprised me after our day together.

Mirabella excused herself as the evening was winding down, and I felt a bit of the trance she seemed to produce in me. When Mirabella appeared at the doorway, much like in Aspen, she seemed to glide into the bedroom, and I was captivated by the sight. My brain spiraled, and I felt dizzy and exhilarated simultaneously. Her spell consumed me.

It was as if we were in our 20s again. No table or chair was omitted from our intimacy, and the hours passed in a blink. The physical part was from another time and place of eternal youth and the strength to make it real. This evening in Quebec City created our relationship's most emotional and intimate moments.

Tonight, she brought an unusual passion. Through our time, Mirabella used her fingernails to create an excitement that was hard to explain. Her nails were always superbly manicured, but my experience evolved tonight in the Chateau. Tonight, her fingernails were an extension of the romantic power she exuded. Tender at times and harsh at others, her fingernails explored every inch of my body and left my skin craving even more. I felt like she had built an energy field around us, and all my nerve endings fired as her nails traced their way around my body.

Time collapsed with Mirabella. The hours passed with energy that continued to build. What was normal for us now extended beyond anything I experienced before. I could feel my body expending itself in ways I never felt before. My legs were dynamic pistons, and my arms coiled and released to hold Mirabella in ways new and exciting.

Mirabella had a scent and taste I had not experienced in our earlier times together. It was as if she "knew" things about our world and ourselves that I had never experienced. In some ways, I was with Gandalf the Grey. In others with the ultimate sensual partner. Where did this woman come from? There was a susurrant voice she used now that was new, at once enticing and riveting. She is a wizard of her art. It was on a level that increasingly became apparent. Art is the only way to describe her actions.

I am enraptured. Nothing exists outside this room, and no one matters other than Mirabella. My life has reduced itself to the here and now. I could easily spend the rest of my life like this.

Mirabella

I almost ruined everything today. As we walked through the town window shopping and laughing, I was suddenly aware of another of my kind nearby. I was transfixed by the feeling. I couldn't move, could barely breathe, and was senseless until Zach pulled me out of it. Had he not, I would have stood there until the other found me and destroyed me. Zach literally saved my life.

This cannot happen again. We need to leave this place. While I would choose to go right now, I need to keep Zach in the dark for a while longer. I was able to distract him during the day, and his mind was swirling with out activities of the night. Tomorrow we will leave according to schedule and this will be a bad memory. I can't wait to get back to New York.

Chapter XVIII

We started the next day in silence. The evening had gone into the morning's light, and our schedule was brutal. We chose to fly back separately—Mirabella to Manhattan and me to the mountain.

On the trip to the small airport, the conversation was short. The mood of the evening was gone replaced now, moving to the "work mode" I had often seen from her. We said our goodbyes in Montreal as we changed terminals for our flights.

Before she left, she asked. "Would you mind coming to Manhattan for a trip to the Met?" The formality of things had changed. Somehow, as we were more intense physically, the emotional separation was greater. Then she gave me one of her Cheek Kisses for the first time since Denver. After our recent events, this seemed a distance-creating moment.

I was not sure what to think.

Our communications during the week seemed odd. Texting seemed to be the preferred Mirabella method now. I missed the sound of her voice. The hypnotic state had now become a text. Not the same.

As the holidays were fast approaching, the subject was taking a toll. I was waiting for Mirabella to express a desire to spend the holidays together or apart. One point of contention was that Mirabella had not mentioned me to her sons. The separation she had kept was intentional as we both were finding our way. Hell, who knew even if there was a way?

Mirabella was quite direct when she mentioned, "We need to discuss the holidays."

"Of course," the holidays will start, and we need to decide what, if anything, we will do," I replied.

There was a firm decision to make about the holidays. Parties, galas, and informal gatherings would now involve me or not. It was as if Mirabella's Manhattan persona was directly involved. By her tone, I was getting the impression from Mirabella that I was a secret. I was part of something past but exciting. I flattered myself by thinking Mirabella wanted to keep me all to herself. Realistically, neither of us knew the direction of our relationship, and she was especially guarding her options. We finally committed to acting when we decided to spend the following weekend at the Metropolitan Museum of Art. There was no question I would go to be with her. Long before, I had given up any personal boundaries. She could twist me like a slinky, and I would say, "Please, ma'am, can I have some more?" I would go. It simply did not matter. I was more than obsessed.

My trip to Manhattan via Westchester was uneventful. The novelty of wide-open spaces and people wearing masks had worn off. I had returned to road warrior mode and was laser-focused on getting to where I wanted to go without delay or detour.

I met Mirabella outside the Museum of Modern Art. The museums of Manhattan are without a peer, and we were on a mission. After a quick cheek kiss, we entered through the patron and owner's entrance by its private door. This doorway helped us avoid the massive crowds ordinarily present. Since this was a Saturday, there were fewer people about.

Mirabella

This weekend is my make-or-break weekend. I need to decide where I am going with Zach. I will expose him to what I am and what I need. I can only hope that the story will scare him off. I'll lay it all out for him and see where we get. I've gotten all that I need from him for now, let's see if I can keep him around for the long term.

MoMA

The Morgan Library & Museum

The Metropolitan Museum of Art- New York City

The firm Mirabella owned is a significant donor, and we could access specific private collections that were not public. Some of the world's largest corporations and international groups were also substantial donors, as giving money to the museum is a highly visible "give back" to the community.

Mirabella and I have visited the Metropolitan before, and the most impressive exhibit may be the Egyptian Temple. It is hard to imagine Manhattan without the comedy and romance portrayed in this special exhibit—the ancient Egyptian temple. The temple was built in the first century BC and gifted to the United States due to the building of the Aswan High Dam. As the dam was made and the water rose, 50 nations worldwide came together to move artifacts in danger of drowning. The Metropolitan received the Temple of Dendur as a monument to the American contribution to the effort. Mirabella had captured me with her knowledge of history and the "collective unconscious" she continued to bring up. The Temple of Dendur is in the Sackler wing, and more importantly, it was in many movies. The backdrop no one can forget.

The Met has been around for 150+ years, and its vision is of the future still leading the way. We were doing the typical tourist exhibits. Then Mirabella suggested we look at the private collections. Some were funded by private investors and dealt with esoteric information. She smiled and enjoyed the surprise she was giving me.

The list of patrons, sponsors, and Donors is beyond the world's financial elite. Where would this lead me?

The E H Wing

Private Collection

During our tour of the main significant exhibits, Mirabella asks:

"Are you aware that several exhibits here are private?"

"I am sure over the past 150 years, there have been mysteries to this building beyond belief," I said.

"They have a private collection that will appeal to you."

Then, as if transported to another time and place, her hypnotic aura appeared around me. Mirabella was taking control, which was a strange, powerful attraction, different from before. Now, the voice in my head was becoming clear. Mirabella was able to control people. I did not know if she used mental abilities, pheromones, or black magic. Mirabella could take over and bend people to her will whenever she chose. No wonder she was such a confident and open conversationalist. No wonder she could make friends with anyone. As I felt my will fading, I realized this was what happened last night and on our previous nights together.

Mirabella introduced me to the mythology and occult wing in a separate museum area. It was not open to the public. The esoteric nature of the presentation would not pass the scrutiny of the present ethos of public display.

Mirabella asked if I could let her be my private tour director.

"Why not"?

Mirabella wanted to show me that the focus of Mythology and Gods from other civilizations was discussed well before the Greeks, Krishna, Allah, Budda, and Sanskrit. Our discussions were detailed because of her time in Europe and her immersion into history from around the world. Mirabella was passionate about going to museums; she had spent much time studying in Europe, and medieval times appealed to her.

Mirabella knew of my interest in esoteric writings back when we met. She tailored her commentary on these exhibits to the paranormal elements they held. She used her knowledge of my interests to provide a blueprint for the experience we were constructing. I was a spiritual person who was on a path with Mirabella as a guide. Her knowledge dovetailed with many of the subjects I studied.

Unknown to me, the massive museum had many rooms not open to the public. Usually, benefactors and significant supporters of the Met had made them possible over the generations. These rooms are dedicated to subjects that may have been of little public interest but defined the scope of the Met by going deeper into specific topics.

"The Metropolitan Museum of Art collects, studies, conserves, and presents significant works of art across time and cultures in order to connect all people to creativity, knowledge, ideas, and one another," said Mirabella. "Many of the cultures of the past created art and artifacts which are unfamiliar or outside of current mores."

When Mirabella discussed her family, it was as if she had first-hand knowledge of the place and times of history. Her ability to transcend time as she debated the exhibits, we viewed was personal, and her visits to European and North American museums made them her home.

She talked to me of the various cultures which used human sacrifice as a method of conversing with the Gods. She spoke to me of cultures that used vision quests, drugs and purification rituals to commune with the heavens. As we walked through the exhibits, we became engulfed in a feeling of time regression. Each artifact pulled us further back to a time when technology and information were simpler and less prevalent. A time when what we consider to be the occult or supernatural was as common as a cell phone.

We spent two days at the Metropolitan. As her story unfolded, she mentioned that myths and legends were often based on facts. The stories were passed on by telling tales, much like the Norse myths. Mirabella took me to a unique private collection.

At the beginning of the second day, Mirabella asked, "Are you aware that humans vary in lifespan and birthing? In many other cultures, people exist that have expanded lifetimes, and they often have elongated times of birth. There are places in Georgian Russia with people living well past 125 years. Science is baffled at times because of this unknown. During my time in Italy, there was a place where my ancestors had a foothold. Sardinia has one of the most extended lifespans on earth. They refer to it in research as a "Blue Zone."

"The blue zones areas of the world share and benefit from a set of habits that we call the Power 9: practices that—together--- increased longevity, health and happiness. Our research has shown that these sets of behaviors and outlooks benefit people in these ways: Longer, healthier life."

Mirabella explained that "storytelling" was a big part of how information flowed from generation to generation in Blue Zone communities. "Truth wrapped in story's garments is easy to behold," she said. We speculated at length as to how lore and longevity related to each other. Of course we talked about the difference between story and myth, the honesty of lore, and how the modern world trivialized ancient wisdom.

She continued with our experience of our own lives in the form of a story. Daily, we fantasize, daydream, write, and continue the change, but we never walk away from the narrative. The purpose of this exhibit was to show that storytelling emerged thousands of years ago as our ancestors began to speak. Oral History may have been memorized and repeated hundreds of times. The sections we visited showed anomalies within humans and world cultures. Mirabella talked about how some life spans are more extended than science knows. We looked at an exhibit describing the *Turritopsis dohrnii,* or immortal jellyfish. A jelly fish that seems to renew itself rather than degrade itself basically making it death proof. We talked of Biblical figures who lived many hundreds of years before death. Were these merely tall tales or did humans actually live so long?

As our day continued, Mirabella explained that it is believed that some blood types and genetics can even keep the "fountain of youth." This allows for triple the lifespan of what we presently consider normal. She knew some Hungarians had a sect she may be related to. The connection was a scarce blood type. The term she used was "Sang." For reference, she described the RHNUL blood type, which is present in less than 1 in 1,000 people.

"My Sang blood type is one thousand times rarer than that," she said.

I noted her comment in the back of my mind as we talked. I paid it no mind as walked and explored. Frankly, I wasn't sure if she was putting me on or if she truly believed that she had some immortal blood type. Time would tell.

One time in Aspen, she mentioned the term, and I had not paid much attention. Now, it seemed to be necessary in our adventure. I tried to store it in my memory, but it slithered away like an eel in oil. Was this part of her "power" over me, or did my mind not have the capacity to understand?

Mirabella explained that while science had advanced the understanding of many things, she reminded me that science used leeches to cure disease as recently as the 1700s. She suggested that I keep an open mind and an inquisitive nature.

Mirabella asked, "Have you ever wondered how the world's various cultures have monuments that look like pyramids? There are more than

100 pyramids in Egypt, and the number in South America and Central America is similar. China, the Balkans, and Thailand all have extensive pyramidical structures dating back thousands of years."

Mirabella seemed fascinated, and now my interest was growing. We discussed various cultures, and we started with the Mayans. The story she wove about the Aztec city of Teotihuacán was that the city's name meant "The place where Gods were created." Mayan culture seemed to be dominated by the city of Teotihuacan. The city is a fantastic display of architecture from ancient times. For a thousand years before the European invasion, men and women traveled to the city to study and became "People of Knowledge."

The city's central road, the Avenue of the Dead, runs south from the Pyramid of the Moon to a large temple complex. The story goes that the conquistadors, who were very accomplished soldiers, marched straight down the avenue and slaughtered the priests in the temples. These men and women were vulnerable to slaughter because they were unwilling to recognize the importance of the conquistadors and offer obeisance.

Mirabella's questions were thought-provoking. How do you communicate the details that created a similar architectural structure of a pyramid in times thousands of years before modern history? Egyptians and other cultures all have pyramids. How did they all gain the knowledge needed to construct such advanced structures? With such knowledge at hand, how did they become extinct.

Mirabella posited the question. "Do you think the ancient man could conceptualize the ideas that created pyramids and mathematics at such a high level? Could they forget it so rapidly that their civilization collapsed?"

"It would not appear logical," I replied. "How did so many cultures worldwide tap into one form of a building?" she asked.

"The shape is not that difficult," I replied. "Pyramids are merely glorified triangles. What interests me is the ability to build such a magnificent structure with "primitive" tools and technology. For example, most people do not know that the Great Pyramid is actually an eight-sided structure. On certain days of the year the shadows show that the sides create an acute angle of their own. At the spring and autumnal equinoxes, the pyramid shows it's true shape."

"I never knew that," said Mirabella. "But it goes to prove my main thesis that our current knowledge is lacking in so many areas. We have forgotten things that we should know and remember. Our paper and electronic records are so ephemeral that without a serious effort to permanently document or knowledge, it will be lost in the next worldwide emergency."

"I think that may be the other piece of the puzzle." I added. "We as a civilization no longer think that "the hand of God" can come down and end a civilization. We all think we are going to live forever and are astonished when we don't."

"Some of us have a different knowledge," said Mirabella.

Chapter XIX

In the E H wing, we saw the art of the world in primitive cultures.

The term she used to describe the constructions was a ziggurat. I was constantly amazed by her use of the English language. She then guided me through a few schools of thought. She explained much like a college professor lecturing a neophyte student.

Atlantis

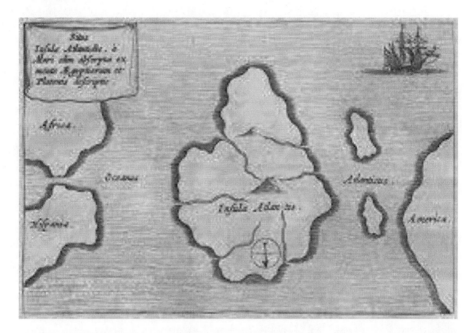

"The story of Atlantis in this room breathes life into the tale. The legend is that Atlantis existed 9000 years before Plato's writings in 360 BC. Atlantis had become a byword for advanced civilizations and the hubris of nations. It seems Atlantis disappeared from the face of the earth. The island was never discovered as the sea was shrouded in mud caused by an earthquake,"

Mirabella said, "It has been suggested that the leaders of the civilizations traveled to the corners of the then-known world, which led to the development of cultures from the Mayans to the Egyptians and northern Europe."

"This is starting to sound a little bit like the Ancient Astronauts Theory," I said. "The next thing we know, we'll be talking about Atlantis, the Pyramids, and interstellar aliens."

"The location of Atlantis is still debated. Many think it was in the middle of what we now call the Atlantic Ocean. Some people believe that the inhabitants of Atlantis still walk amongst us. I have met several. Trust me, they are not all that special," she said.

This comment struck me as odd. Why would she say she'd met people from Atlantis? How would she know? Where the Atlanteans physically different? Did they exude some special aura that she could see? Why would she even think that people from a civilization extinct for thousands of years would still be around?

Or, was she referring to herself? Was she from Atlantis thousands of years ago. Maybe she was the child of an Atlantean. My mind flipped back to our weekend in Canada and her strange actions on the street when she seemed to stall like a statue. Was this some affect of Atlanteans?

My back tingled as I thought these thoughts. Then I remembered the scratches I spotted after every visit with Mirabella. Was she marking me in some way? Would I be recognizable to Atlanteans as "one of them" going forward? Had she infected me with some Atlantean recognition symbol or germ? These and a thousand other questions swirled in my brain as Mirabella continued her lecture.

In her mystical way, Mirabella then directed the conversation about history being considered a myth and legend. She asked, "Have you ever heard of the Jewish philosopher Philo?"

The Jewish philosopher Philo wrote about the destruction of Atlantis. The island was greater than Africa and Asia, and the earthquake overwhelmed Atlantis and sank it beneath the sea.

THE BOOK

A copy of the book "Atlantis" by Ignatius Donnelly from 1882 is exhibited, showing widespread interest in Atlantis. Although considered pseudoarcheology, this book purported that ancient civilizations were descended from more advanced beings. The book drew parallels between the creation stories in the bible and significant religious works. The writer believed myths hold information that may have unique insight into human development. Culture is more scientifically advanced and possibly more sophisticated in its manner. A great flood may have destroyed it.

Another summary we read was that the civilization of Atlantis reached its peak 1 million years ago but destroyed itself through internal warfare. The inhabitants of Atlantis had mighty psychic and supernatural powers, said Mirabella.

We discussed Myths and Legends, their power, and how oral histories are passed down before the written word. How could they all be just fabrications?

Mirabella thought not.

"How do we learn?" she asked.

She said that from nursery rhyme stories to intricate details of novels, it is by repetition and storytelling. Mirabella had been educating me for some time. Her story was that things are not easily explained beyond the legends. Mirabella continued.

"Could it be that the people of the earth were populated and had different visitors among us?"

Theories of Atlantis leaders going to the earth's far reaches to create, educate, and populate an educated race to raise this planet's intelligence level. Mirabella made note of how intelligence morphs into conventional wisdom. Her comments were in passing, but her comment made sense to me. She continued:

"The purpose of which may be unknown to "mere mortals." I am sure she was referring to my taking in her view of the world.

"What if people are walking among us from other worlds?" she proposed.

Intrigued, I asked, "How would anyone know?"

"Have you noticed how technology is morphing into ways never before conceived? Artificial intelligence, machine learning, genetics, pharmacology, healthcare, physics, and robotics are changing the world as we are in this room.

She smiled her coy smile and mentioned a term I heard her use in Aspen, Sang.

"I was hoping you could take some time with the paintings in this Hall." Sangs" were a topic of several of the pictures. The concept of others from beyond our day-to-day human experience is intriguing. Astrophysics has explained this in many books as an example of the hubris of man thinking he understands the universe.

Suddenly it all came together. The little voice in my head was screaming at the top of it's lungs. "She's a Sang!" Now it has become clear.

The exhibits of the Sang culture coordinated their existence with the Atlantean myth. Noone knew where they came from originally, but the Atlantean culture was well aware of the Sang. They were revered as healers and seers. Sang coexisted with humans in Atlantis and throughout the Atlantean empire. Legends of Sang "adopting" humans and using their blood to extend the Sang lifetime were prominently displayed in the literature. Modern scientists dismissed these legends as myths and/or fairy tales. Some researchers pointed to Sang as the origin of Vampire and Skinwalker legends.

I studied Mirabella out of the corner of my eye as she continued my education. Now that I knew what I was looking for, it was more obvious that she was not entirely human.

How can a mortal man understand the cosmos?

Mirabella was discussing intelligence, or rather that the guardians of other worlds would guide humans to a flexible intelligence unbound by any precedent.

In Aspen, she mentioned the term "Sang." Suddenly, my weeks of thinking and consideration came together. The fog in my mind around her use of the term Sang suddenly lifted In the exhibit hall. I had to ask. "Mirabella, my love, are you different from most of us? Is this your way of telling me that you are some timeless being who lives forever on the blood of humans?"

My words stunned me because I immediately realized their truth. All the puzzle pieces snapped into place with a boom in my head. The brain fog I felt when I was with her, the electrical field when we were making love, and the familiarity with times and places from the past all rushed together to shatter my sense of being and understanding. My passion from my past was from much farther in the past than I had thought. How could this be? How could I know Mirabella so well, yet not at all?

I was gob smacked. Then, my rational mind took over again. Mirabella was unique. Was she human? Did the families she mentioned in Hungary and Italy exist? Were there more like her out in our world?

Mirabella smiled an intimate smile, giving me time to sort through my feelings and shock.

I was intrigued by her. Her body was that of a 28-year-old. She could take years off her face with only a makeup touch-up. Or was she? Was she even human? Was she distorting herself in my eyes by some power or ability? How could I know? Anything I thought I knew was now tainted by the possibility that she was manipulating my perception of her and our joined reality. She gave me a coy smile.

Rather than a direct answer, she told me what may have been mythology or reality and her belief in esoteric knowledge. She began as we approached a painting from the Renaissance period: "The Opening of the Fifth Seal" by El Greco.

"Domenico's was a dear," she said. "He constantly tried to pretend to be more than he could be. He died quickly of some illness. I was out of town at the time. By the time I heard he was sick and got back, he'd been buried for two weeks."

I looked at her in amazement. Without saying a word, Mirabella had confessed to being a non-human being, hundreds of years old, and familiar with many times and places in antiquity.

The myth as she explained it to me goes a little like this: "Sang" are the aristocracy of the "sangs of the Greek legends" and used sweet sounds that lured men to their deaths. Modern man refers to them as Sirens. A woman was seductive or beautiful, and the detail of being a Sang became more accurate. The Sang appeared in legend and were connected to other dark forces, including those of the nonmortals.

She told of a theory that many lived among us and are older than science has led us to believe. Mirabella said that in her experience, many such beings existed. She used the analogy of diversity in humans.

She mused, "I always thought I was a bit different."

Mirabella described what she had learned from her world travels. She commented on her travels from Hungary to Switzerland to the United Kingdom and the prominent legends of every culture.

I had to ask. "Mirabella, you have mentioned "Sang" more than once in the last six months. Where are you going with that? Are you a Sang?"

She smiled and explained with the same hypnotic effect I had been accustomed to.

"In Hungary, I was told about a myth. Did you know that one can only be born a Sang? You can't become a Sang. What is it Lady GaGa sings? "I was born this way."

"But how can you be born Sang when Sang were/are Atlantean? Does Sang reproduction continue for centuries? Why haven't Sang completely populated the earth?"

I wondered, "What am I hearing." Indeed,

The picture she painted for me was of a universal image of many pictures within one canvas, making it more straightforward. By birth and with a unique blood type, the Sang are an elite group that has continued worldwide. The fuel for the Sang was three drops of human blood per year to perpetuate human development. This blood allowed continued reproduction and nearly endless life.

Mirabella had more in-depth views. One Greek myth involves a special kind of woman. She began to discuss the Sang.

Sang

Mirabella explained while pointing at the painting.

"Sang were those beings who wooed men and needed blood to renew their bodies, and with longer life spans, a source of energy was needed. Sang usually ended their own lives. It seems we are burdened by the reality of living as a young person for generations."

"I can imagine that Sang would grow bored with life, but it seems rather drastic to take one's own life."

While the story of Dorian Gray was the first thing on my mind, the questions were becoming more personal and intense. In the story, Dorian Gray sold his soul for eternal youth. His picture aged with time, but Dorian did not. Finally he could no longer stand the aged look of the picture and destroyed it, destroying himself with it.

"Mirabella, was Oscar Wilde Sang?"

She nodded. "Aging is not part of the process; usually, only a drop or two of blood is necessary to keep the energy high. Oscar stopped taking the blood of Reginald Turner when he was in prison. As a result he died of encephalomeningitis. I was with him that final day. Such a tragedy."

The mention of blood made me feel uneasy about being in another world. The many occasions of intimacy with Mirabella rushed into my mind and provided a foundation for the growing fear in the back of my mind. I remembered her comment about seeming to have scratched me and our intense physical activities.

We stopped before "Hercules and the Sangs" by Christopher Wood as Mirabella continued her revelations. "The version of the movies and books is no more than a Fairy tale about those known as the "living dead" or, more precisely, Voodoo.

She continued to make references to "Sangs."

"Sangs" can have children with mortals; sometimes, there is a skip in a generation. The Sang gestation period is a minimum of three years. The mother must move often to avoid suspicion. Fortunately, the gestation period provides the mother with many protections for her health. Sang mothers can stand privations that humans cannot. They can survive without food or water for years, with just a few drops of blood every year."

"Have you been harvesting my blood?" I asked her directly.

"Yes I have."

Secrets continued. Mirabella mentioned her mother in many different stories. She was having a little fun with me but continued speaking about her family.

Mirabella had a significant attachment to her mother. Her mother's fears were confirmed as she knew her daughter was of a time and place that haunted every third generation and only the female side. Her mother was very conservative and feared the disclosure of an unusual daughter in the small town where she lived. She was fearful of the Church. She was afraid of the government. But, most of all, she was terrified of her daughter.

"My mother worried that I would be scooped up by people who wanted to experiment on me and find out the secrets of our longevity. She moved all across Europe until I was born. Then, she settled in Hungary. I've told you about that."

It was a point of pride as the aristocracy of her "Sang" heritage was easy to see. Her movements and vast knowledge of history brought things to and beyond my understanding.

Mirabella

So far, he is taking it well. I'm barely using any of my misdirection powers or my suppression skills. He's drawing the right conclusions and asking the right questions. So like Jacob all those years ago. If only our blood hadn't been so incompatible. But then, that was always one of the attractions of Jacob. The fact that should I grow weary of this world, I could leave it with my husband's blood in my veins. As it turned out, he left the world with my blood in his veins. Equally deadly. Our boys will go through life with the two bloodlines battling within them until one triumphs and the other converts. I hope I'm here to see the results.

Mirabella knew her attractions and why. I had been a close presence once. For some reason, she could think of no one else during the plague. It was an odd fascination she'd had during her time with me. The attraction from the past was locked in her mind. Blood types were vitally important in her culture. She remembered I had a unique blood type called a "slayer." Slayers were the only thing that could undo the spells and ultimately end the life of a sang. It was an attraction that did not quickly leave her mind.

Mirabella explained that her heritage made her condition clear to those who knew the story. Over the years, there was the inevitable breeding among the soldiers who occupied the territory throughout the constant wars, the locals, and the elite. There was a fine line between hiding from the authorities and living a "normal" life. Mirabella had survived for centuries on her wit, charm, and luck.

Because she was unique in blood type, her body had a fantastic quality of never being ill. It was strange for her mother and family to realize her uniqueness as one of the chosen, and to ostracize her was part of the fear from the first generation of Hungarians in America, making it palpable.

Her need for blood only needed a drop or two every six months now. Over the years, the need had grown. Mirabella obtained this as a child from her mother, and it was their secret. It was a constant reminder of their connection. The rift between them was genetic. Mirabella had a rare blood type only found in one line of her family. The blood made the first-generation Italians suspect many things about her behavior and future. Mirabella had a choice of protecting her family or letting the mystery come out into an unforgiving world. That could never happen. Her choice was to leave her family and wander the world alone. She would return every few decades to check on the family and reacquaint herself with her roots. Otherwise, she went where the currents of time and space took her.

The day was ending, and we were still in the Met. I was suffering from information overload combined with the most interesting and exciting time of my life. I was more than a little unsure of my reality.

The Stanhope

After the exhaustion of the day, we both needed food and refreshments. The Stanhope was close by. It had, on this day, the outside veranda for cocktails. We sat, smiled, and decided to take the evening to a less frantic place of fantasy information. A wonderful day with laughter and joy, she seemed to only continue with her fantastic ability to be comfortable in any situation as she enchanted the staff. We spent the remainder of the afternoon verbally dancing around the revelations of the day.

She mentioned that "Checking in for Tea at the Stanhope" is another reference to a Manhattan story. Years before, we had met there on occasion. It seemed an excellent way to end the afternoon.

The Evening Back in the Apartment

That evening, Mirabella brought even more surprises. Safely ensconced in the apartment, we ordered in for dinner.

Mirabella thought-

"How much should I share now that we are transgressing on my original intentions? I dropped many subtle hints in the Met today and a few direct statements. Could he figure out the solution to the puzzle? It would be best to do the question-and-answer thing that had worked for decades."

Mirabella asks me:

"Do you think those myths and legends have any basis in reality? Think of what we saw today—the stories from thousands of years ago."

While the discussion started with a fun atmosphere of wine and food, she was moving in a different direction.

Mirabella thought-

The myths and legends are more accurate when you know the Sang from the tales were real. They had a beauty and voice that called many to their deaths. The aristocracy of the occult, the Sang, have lifespans of 500 or more years. It could be longer, but the passing of children and relationships complicated our existence as technology continued its identification path.

Sang typically reach a point where a formal process would quickly end their existence when they were sure of continuance into other generations. When a Sang knew their genes would continue without them, when time had worn down their veneer of life, the Sang would seek out a slayer and undo the spells that bound them to this world. After, they would live and age naturally to their final journey.

Mirabella prospered financially and physically through working with various countries and making continued younger relationships. Sang had one weakness: they could easily mate with humans. Their unique blood type was not often transferred, making it necessary to keep new men alive and in her life.

While in Aspen, I had nicked Zach's ear and took a single drop of his blood. This taste of him brought back why he was here now. Zach was a mortal, and he was 54. He could not be a long-term partner as some before him had been.

Zach had a unique blood type. As a "Slayer," he greatly attracted me as a Sang. It was as if the appeal was physical but fearful of the consequences. My last husband succumbed when my blood was shared in a confused rush to a hospital. A first rule of her kind not to break. She knew that the transference of blood from a Sang to normal humans

171

would result in an internal battle between the human white cells and those of the Sang. Even one drop of the Sang's cells quickly overwhelmed the human's cells, causing the human's death.

The Zack conundrum continued as he had the unique blood type of a slayer. Mirabella only needed a few drops of blood during the month. Those three drops were essential. As her age increased, so did the need for and quantity of blood. As a child, she could live on three drops of blood per year. Now, she needed that amount monthly. Soon, it would be weekly and, ultimately, daily. She did not know what would happen after that. Having Zach nearby when the time came would be helpful. But was the time coming now? Had she truly become world-weary and ready for the sweet release of an easy death?

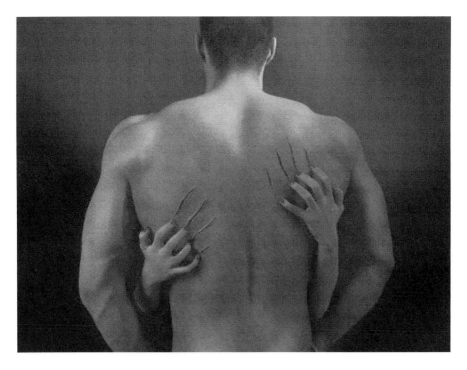

Sang need to feed on human blood. They are the ultimate aristocrat of this world, as no country or boundary binds them. Zach may accept me

now, but it would mean we would start a meaningful relationship. With life extending beyond any time frame wishes, I must think of decades rather than years and balance that against my lust for life.

The power of the evening was now reaching back to the first times. Mirabella was a force when it suited her. She expressed herself in a physical way that was not of this world. The touch, the taste, her smell, and her beauty all came together. It was a sign that I could not resist. Our evening ended early the following day. After jumping into sweats and catching a car to Westchester, I noticed an itching that was not painful. Just irritating.

Chapter XX

It Ended

As it Began, with a text.

After a long holiday from Thanksgiving to January, the intensity of the budding relationship between Mirabella and I came to the point of no return.

I saw the words and knew that as things started with an electron beam, it now was reduced to:

"Hey... sorry... work and life has gotten a little complicated."

Complicated in Aspen and Manhattan have the same meaning. It was simply over. Neither of us ever made or tried to communicate further.

I pondered my time with Mirabella. I am convinced she is Sang. She is a being not of time or space but of the ethereal. Why had she chosen me, twice? What did I have that attracted and held her? I thought of all the things she told me and finally settled on blood.

She used me to satisfy some blood lust or need in her physical existence. Had I fulfilled the role of Reginald Turner for Mirabella? She admitted to harvesting my blood. I knew of the effect she had on my physical and mental well-being and how the Sang used their extra usual powers to control humans. Had I fallen under that spell?

ONE YEAR LATER

I had an older brother. He was a military man in the U.S. Army for 30 years. He was 12 years older than me, and we were not as close as brothers should be. TJ, as he was known, was a great athlete. He played basketball in both college and the Army. He died, and I arranged his funeral and burial.

The past eight months were the most meaningful of our relationship between brothers. Our youngest brother, Evan, died, possibly by his own hand. TJ was buried in a plot at the same church where he had been married. The two brothers would spend eternity side by side.

Reflecting on our last month's together, TJ and I had never related more, and I got to know him as the man he became. He visited the mountains, and we spent an afternoon together, having lunch and talking. We talked for an hour on the day he died, and I have never enjoyed our conversation more. He was optimistic and happy. He spoke of things we shared as children and his life in the military, the meaningless posts, the corruption, the ineptitude, and the brilliant, exhilarating feeling of serving your country. He lived for five years in Hawaii and was grateful for that time. His son, wife, and grandchildren made the graveside service a meaningful experience for me.

As was my custom, I placed a traveler with those who predeceased me. The traveler at this moment was a pocket watch that our father wore. He owned a construction company, and this watch never left him. The "traveler" was a show of our bloodline continuance.

My brother knew my dad in a way that I did not. He may have suffered from being the firstborn, but he was always our mother's favorite. Or so my other brother and I believed. He lived a well-lived life. He was not compromised by an overwhelming intellect but had a profound sense of being.

So, as it began when I went to TJ's wedding, it ended at the same place. A life of 30 years of service to his country, and here lies a man I respected.

THE REQUEST

As the service ended, I received an unusual request from Carolyn, my brother's wife, who asked me to do a DNA saliva test. I thought about this for a few moments and then consented. She was a devotee of Ancestry and wanted to trace the family history. She would probably not stumble onto the family's roots in the 1600s.

I thought nothing more of the request.

The Surprise

The weeks passed, and I thought no more about the funeral. The time for grieving had passed.

Months later, Carolyn called late one evening. The surprise was that Carolyn had never called before. Carolyn told me that her family was English, and she could trace people and events to the 1700s. It was a little close for me, but I had another 100 years before she could have learned about the Lord Proprietors. Carolyn's tone conveyed she had probably reached the end of her need for research.

Carolyn and I shared a unique relationship. My brother was in the Army, and when she was pregnant with my nephew, I went to the hospital the day he was born. My mother "Ms. Helen," had commanded my presence, and no one ever denied her. From that day forward, Carolyn would call or write on infrequent occasions. She kept me informed of the major life activities in their life. I never pressed out of respect for TJ.

As Carolyn was discussing family lineage, she asked me a unique question.

"Something showed up in your DNA test that may or may not be applicable. It seems you have a unique blood type. While I know you have three sons, is there any chance you are connected to anyone in Hawaii?"

"Nope, I have only been there three times in my life. To my knowledge, only your clan has lived there.

Carolyn said, "I have some information. I am not sure what it means?"

It seemed Carolyn was being cautious in making her comments.

Eventually, I said, "Carolyn, what are you saying?"

"As you know, I have been researching Ancestry and several other sites. While I don't know about DNA testing, you have what may be considered a surprise."

"I'm somewhat lost at this point; what are we discussing here?"

Carolyn said, "Your blood type has matched a man in his 30s. He lives in Hawaii and is a medical doctor."

Beyond Comprehension

Sitting in my office and talking to Carolyn became surreal. The questions seemed to me to be about a supernatural experience. Finding out about a potential son who had been spirited away was not from my world. Was this child Mine and Mirabella's?

If so, why would Mirabella make such a decision?

Her wedding had been a charade of some sort. My invitation had always puzzled me. It was not logical given our relationship, yet we had spent a year dating and traveling. It was puzzling to recall her actions. Jacob was clearly infatuated with Mirabella, and Mirabella did not appear to be pregnant. With my added insight, it is possible that she was hiding the pregnancy. I wished I asked Mirabella more about the gestation process. Had Mirabella used Jacob as a front for her pregnancy with me? If so, why not just tell me of the pregnancy and then determine our options and way forward?

If she'd carried my child for three years, how had it escaped Jacob's notice? If she was a year into her pregnancy, she might not have looked the part. She could easily have controlled Jacob with her "powers" to blind him to the length of the gestation period. Mirabella should have considered at least a phone call. The deception of the past year made it even more challenging to understand.

The scenario of her wedding came back into focus. Mirabella must have known this ceremony was in some way for us. Given the explanation she mentioned in The Metropolitan Museum of Art, her sect had an extremely long gestation period, and now it was becoming more apparent. She was not of the everyday world. She was, in fact, a "Sang." This 30-year secret was now known by two.

Surely, it was worth a phone call.

The wonder of the legacy this young man had and would never be aware of was fantastic. Who was he? What drives did he have to become a

Medical Doctor? The absence of knowing him and what could have been are tectonic shocks to my soul.

Then, all things started to come together.

Mirabella had asked me to go to her wedding.

Now, it was confirmed that she was pregnant at the time. The reason for the invitation was the need to bind us in a way beyond my understanding. At the time, I thought how strange this was. Now, it made sense in a Mirabella sort of way.

Later

I continued my business trips to Manhattan. Ayn Rand had told the world that this was the epicenter of Capitalism. The trust and the foundations of which I was a board member had New York offices and required visits occasionally. I used my spare time in New York to visit the museum and delve deeply into all things Sang. I read the Atlantis stories, I read blood line and blood type data relating to Sang and Humans. I read accounts of Sang and human relationships and how the various blood combinations worked or didn't. Finally, I pieced together the story that made sense to me. Did it make sense to Mirabella?

My blood type was a unique type even amongst the Sang. They called it a Slayer type. The blood could keep Sang alive for centuries with adequate use. The problem for the Sang lay in the fact that Slayer blood, in greater quantities, could kill a Sang. Sang would seek out a Slayer when they became tired of the world. They would take excessive quantities of Slayer blood and pass on. Some Sang would expire peacefully, some would suffer exquisite pain and agony from the reaction. Regardless, the Slayer option was the only way to complete a Sang life. The knowledge consumed me and forced me to consider what Mirabella wanted from our first, and second relationship. The need to know grew in my mind like a cancer requiring excision.

I became determined to visit Mirabella's Sutton Place apartment during one stay.

Why? I had no clue.

What would be said, and what would be the determination of events? My thoughts ran from a confrontation of the secret to the year-long involvement. Emotional as it all was, it developed into an obsession.

Sutton Place

The car to Sutton Place from the Pierre was a short ride. Winter was always the best time to be in Manhattan. I was gearing up for a conversation that may not be appropriate if it happened at all.

Upon arrival at Sutton Place, I met a different doorman. The present gatekeeper said the former doorman had retired and moved to upstate New York. When I asked him if Ms. Mirabella was available, he said he was unaware of anyone living in the building by that name.

I nodded in understanding. Mirabella was gone.

She and the doorman disappeared. I thought about how that was right. She left and sent the doorman into retirement so no one could notice her continuing agelessness. I had an eerie feeling as I left Sutton Place. I knew that secrets of the past were still there, but I could not shake the feeling that something sinister was lurking inside those walls. The doorman's disappearance further proved that something wasn't right. I couldn't help but wonder what happened to Mirabella.

I wondered if my conversation would have changed anything or if it was best that I left things alone. It seemed that certain secrets were better off left unsolved - the only thing I could do now was move on and hope everyone involved stayed safe.

While waiting for my car, I thought back over the past year and one year 25 years ago that can never be replicated or forgotten. My drive back to the Pierre brought memories of the cities that now would forever be ingrained in my soul. My thoughts returned to the mountain as I drove away from Sutton Place. I anticipated seeing the smile on Rachel's face when I arrived home.

Sometimes, adventures need to be left alone.

Mirabella

Zach will never know about his role in the continuation of the Sang. Our first child is doing well in Hawaii. He became a doctor unaware of the miracle of his own birth and lineage. It hurt to turn him over to the foster authorities, but even Jacob couldn't ignore the fact that she was pregnant when they married. Her ability to control Jacob made the situation easier, but she still wished she could have done a better job in the situation.

My son is married and has children. The Sang line continues. His line will mix with other human genes and blood types to diversify Sang genetics. A closed chapter. Now a new chapter is beginning. Zach's second child is growing slowly within me. I will travel the world for the next two years until the child is ready. My business and personal wealth is sufficient to allow me to travel in style. The child within will keep me safe from illness as we travel, and I will make sure the child has a safe and comfortable start to their life.

I often wonder if I have done the right thing by using Zach the way I have. Does he know that I used him so blatantly? Does he care? I'll never know as we will never meet again. When the child is born, I will consider how much longer this world will hold interest for me. With the speed of technology, it won't be long before mankind goes to the planets and stars. Do I want to go with them? Do I want to spread Sang to the universe? We'll see. For now, I am just an expectant mother traveling the world until she starts raising her child.

What could be more normal?

Rachel, my housekeeper, tried hard to be on time. She always did, but there was a little game between her and I. Rachel always showed up 15 minutes late, no matter what. I always told her to be there 15 minutes ahead of time.

Rachel had come into my life after the death of my wife, Leigh. Leigh came down with one of those diseases with no cure, and her quick passing left a void in my life. Leigh died early, but I was left with the love of my life, my daughter Elizabeth. Elizabeth, the child of my first marriage at 18, was now an adult and married, which was her life course. I was a little lonely, but it was always an adventure with Elizabeth and her husband, James. It also seemed there was a baby on the way.

"There he is," she thought.

Rachel thought her 54-year-old boss was suffering depression from the loss of a long-term mate and transitioning to his new life without his daily breakfasts with his daughter.

But Rachel wondered why Mr. Zach appeared in such a good mood lately, and then she realized something was going on as he had scheduled a trip to Denver. Why was his demeanor upbeat? She could only guess why. The pandemic raged worldwide. The nightly news was as depressing as she had ever heard it. Thirty-six-year-old Rachel was between two of her many careers. Something always went wrong for Rachel in the 8-5 jobs she held. Recently, Rachel had to move back in with her mother, and her mother constantly made her aware that Zach would be a catch for her. Rachel was not seeing or feeling it. Zach had to be in his 50s, and she still enjoyed her occasional young man.

My morning was going south fast. Rachel was late as usual, and it's her habit. I guess I could make an issue of it, but Rachel was a reliable worker, and Charlie loved her. Charlie, my golden retriever, greeted Rachel. Charlie could charm the devil- his smile and dog face reminded me how fast things can change. A few months ago, I was dogless. I can't imagine a day without his goofy smile or the energy he brings to the household. In a few short years, he would be gone. Maybe Charlie will be replaced by another homeless animal looking for love. The process repeats many times in a person's lifetime, but only once for the dog.

I waited for my driver to take me to my helipad. The AW119kx was waiting. The helicopter flight to the international airport was only 24 minutes. I live on one of the highest mountains in the Appalachian

Mountain range. I use the helicopter for my East Coast travels and could only think of one thing at the moment:

I was seeing Mirabella.

I live in my family's mansion. The house was an appropriate lodge style. The views are unbelievable and within a gated community. I protected my 26-acre estate with a security group. I enjoy sunrises over the Mountain and spectacular sunsets with sunny day views of Charlotte, the South's most gracious city. Over the years, I added amenities, including a 9-hole golf course and a heated Olympic pool. The original home had been razed long ago, and the estate was not included in state or county real estate appraisals. This is another benefit of my heritage. The enhancements continued with a 345-degree view of the peaks in the Blue Ridge mountains. A two-story waterfall also graced the entrance to the home with a 3000 square foot party pavilion and guest house. I took pride in my home.

Inside my home, the woodwork is intricate with cypress paneling, poplar, and cherry that complement the intricate stone masonry. The lodge has a 25-foot-high timber-framed great room, an enhanced gourmet kitchen with custom cabinets, and a mesquite dining table. The reading room, my favorite place, resembled the Vanderbilt's library in Asheville. The mountain was a family gift, as was the surrounding territory handed down for generations.

Still, the landholdings were immense through trust and territorial agreements. The English Lord Proprietors had established ownership with the King of England, and the land grant from King Charles was massive. The Lord Proprietors were eight Englishmen to whom King

Charles II granted, by the Carolina charters of 1663 and 1665, the joint ownership of a tract of land in the New World called "Carolina." George, his sixth great-grandfather, had been the only person who retained title to the land awarded, so the name and family acquired a vast tract of land in perpetuity. My family received an allodial title gifted to his family for all time. Many areas listed officially as government-owned are part of my family's landholdings. The lands stretch from the Atlantic to the Pacific.

The Carolinas, now marked North and South Carolina, have three distinct areas: "the Coastal Plain, Piedmont, and the Mountains. I had chosen the highest point in the Appalachians to view the land for my home. While remote, it had all the available amenities and served the purpose of having few visitors.

Today, my thoughts were only on one thing.

I was seeing Mirabella.